CANNIBAL GOLD

CANNIBAL GOLD

BAD TIMES BOOK ONE

CHUCK DIXON

L M B P N

DISRUPTIVE IMAGINATION

Copyright © 2019 (as revised) Chuck Dixon
Cover Art by Jake @ J Caleb Design
http://jcalebdesign.com / jcalebdesign@gmail.com
Cover copyright © LMBPN Publishing

LMBPN Publishing
PMB 196, 2540 South Maryland Pkwy
Las Vegas, NV 89109

Version 1.10, May 2020
eBook ISBN: 978-1-64202-842-3
Print ISBN: 978-1-64202-843-0

DWAYNE ROENBACH

D wayne hated his job but loved the money.

He was making a tax-free five grand a week and all the perks that came with guarding a guy with a gross worth of just under two billion.

Travel. Fine food. Even if he ate in the kitchen, it was the same stuff they were serving in the formal dining room. And a clothing allowance that netted him a closet loaded with only the best threads. Not bad for a guy who never made better than E-8 after ten years in the Rangers.

The only downside was the boss was a royal asshole. He was one of those bastards lucky enough to be born into money and smart enough to increase the pile by a factor of ten with real estate, part ownership in an NFL team, a chain of car dealerships and a dozen hospitals. The guy woke up every day a few million richer without ever lifting a finger. All the dude did was party here and party there in his off-time, and his whole life was off-time. Wheels up for his private jet at a moment's notice and Dwayne tagged along with the personal chef, personal trainer, and the personal life coach.

Dwayne's function was personal protection.

The boss referred to him as "my samurai."

The guy had no real enemies. He was no high-profile high-roller. As much of a prick as he was, he never screwed anyone over and wasn't particularly political. But he wanted muscle nearby, and Dwayne had the cred and sure looked the part with his Ranger muscle, 6'4" height, 20" neck, desert squint, and fast hands. The guy hired Dwayne away from Sullivan Security Systems where he had been working mostly casino security for Sullivan in Biloxi. It was secure but thankless work.

The work was a breeze. Just look frosty. Be close when the boss wanted and vanish when he didn't. Maybe the boss thought Dwayne would be handy if any shit ever *did* hit the fan. Maybe guys with money just want to live longer to enjoy it. Dwayne couldn't fault him for that. Only why would you want to live a longer life if you had to spend it as an asshole? But then assholes didn't see themselves that way.

Dwayne could have cruised to forty and retired with all the cash he squirreled away. Maybe buy a gas station or a laundromat back in Pensacola. Would have been sweet.

Until that night at Bellagio when the boss coldcocked the cocktail waitress.

The boss was losing big at an exclusive hold 'em table in a room set aside for money guys. A punk who hosted a hit cable reality show was at the other end of the table and roostering after a series of hot hands. He snickered every time the boss blew a call and made remarks to the pretty boy seated next to him, then they'd both titter. The boss's chips went from a wall of stacks to a piddly pile. It wasn't the money he was losing that was torqueing him. Every cent on the table wouldn't keep him in socks for six months. What did *that* matter? It was the fey punk in his kiss-my-ass hat and celebutard mouth that was rubbing the boss the wrong way. A weak attempt at macho had the boss going all-in on a pair of tens and losing the pile to the braying punk.

On the way from the room, he took it out on the poor

redhead whose only mistake was holding a tray of comp apple-tinis and offering them to the wrong guy at the wrong time. He drove a fist into her face hard enough to send a false eyelash airborne. The girl, all hundred pounds of her, went down to the carpet in a spray of vodka.

The boss crouched over her with his face red and lips twisted. He cocked his fist back for a second shot, but Dwayne snatched his wrist and easily held the punch in place. Casino security was there but looking everywhere else. You spend enough money and you get a lot of leeway on this floor.

"That's enough, Jefe," said Dwayne.

"No one touches me," said the boss.

"For your own good," said Dwayne.

"You let me go, or I'll fire you."

"You'll thank me in the morning."

"You'll be gone in the morning," said the boss. "You'll be gone, and you'll be ruined. No one will hire you. I'll make sure of it. You'll be working at—"

Dwayne never did hear where he'd be employed in the future because the next sound the boss made was a high-pitched animal squeal when his elbow was suddenly turned the wrong way around. That ended in a gasp when Dwayne twisted the arm farther and the shoulder separated with a pop you could hear over the slots clanging.

Security stepped up and dragged Dwayne to the deck. And then more security. The Vegas cops were called. Dwayne came around in the back of a police cruiser. No one ever told him how many real cops and rent-a-cops it took to get him there. His best guess was that they were at company strength.

The sweet life was over and there was no going back.

He'd banked thirty grand, but half of that had gone to a lawyer who got his case dismissed. And he'd run through the rest fast enough unless a paying job came up soon. The dwindling bank balance and the clothes on his back were all he had. Everything else was back at the boss's house in Malibu, and he wasn't going there again. The restraining order made sure of that.

Dwayne camped at a sixty-bucks-a-night trucker's hotel out on the 15 near Nellis. He bought some clothes at a big 'n' tall and picked up a *Car Trader* to find a new ride, but that just made him think about the H2 and the Viper the boss used to let him borrow. Mostly he drank beers and sunned by the scummy pool out back of the motel and listened to the heavies flying overhead to and from the miles-long strips at the airbase a few miles north. Took him back to Kandahar when his only worry was an IED. Now he had real shit on his mind. Like the rest of his life. He lay there and sucked back on his Coors and sniffed the air, rich with the tang of high octane aviation fuel cast off by the traffic booming into Nellis overhead.

A lot of days went by like that. Easy and slow.

The nights were longer. He was dating a waitress at the Hooters on Tropicana. But she started giving him shit about getting a job, so he cut that off. She was part of his downtime. He didn't need to hear how he fucked up when he was trying to forget exactly that.

So he had plenty of spare time to review the facts and weigh his options. He'd fucked himself out of a golden opportunity. Really, truly fucked himself. A phone call to Sullivan confirmed that. Danny Sullivan told Dwayne he was blackballed, burned, and generally filed under bad news.

The boss had seen to that. No one would touch him now. And if Dwayne pushed it there was a phony statutory rape charge hanging fire back in Mississippi. Not even the outfits that prided themselves on being bad boys would touch him—the ones with foreign contracts to watch over oil fields or mining operations. Dwayne even thought about re-upping for Rangers, or maybe even regular army. He could easily be an instructor at Benning or elsewhere. He put that decision off till he was down to five large in the checking account. He'd pissed in his own pool and had no one to blame but himself.

He ran ten miles every morning before the sun came up. A shower, shit, and shave, and he walked across the parking lot to the IHOP for coffee and eggs. He was avoiding Hooters for now. Dwayne was in his usual booth studying the *Car Trader* and sipping his second refill. The *Trader* was two months old by now and most of the cars probably sold. He only brought it so he'd have somewhere to look while he ate. Someone slid onto the bench seat across from him.

"Dwayne Tyler Roenbach?" asked the man. "Not if you're a lawyer," Dwayne replied. He didn't look up. *2008 Chev Avlnche. Lw milge. 350. 4wd. BO*

The man laughed, then stopped when Dwayne didn't join him.

"Pat Mulroy suggested I see you," the man said. He was on the underfed side and peered at Dwayne from behind eyeglasses. His hands looked soft and they twitched on the tabletop.

"Where do you know Pat from?" Dwayne folded the *Car Trader* closed.

"He was a consultant on some government projects I was working on," the man said. "I'm private sector now but when I had need of a certain kind of help I contacted Pat."

"How is he?"

"If you know Pat, then you know he never says how he is. Or where he is."

Dwayne knew. That is, he knew that no one knew much about Patrick Mulroy that Mulroy didn't want them to know.

"He said you were a big help to him a few years ago," the man continued.

Peshawar. One evil night. Mulroy was in the kind of corner that only a platoon of Rangers could get him out of. They left half the unit behind that night. And ten times that number of jihadis.

"So, let's cut the shit and the mini-moves," said Dwayne. "Who are you?"

"I'm Dr. Morris Tauber, and I need—"

"Someone who can keep their head when it turns nasty," Dwayne finished for him.

"To put a finer point on it, Mr. Roenbach." Tauber's nervous smile evaporated. "I need a man who can take a small team into the most dangerous place on the planet and bring all of them back alive. No back-up. No support. No communications. There and back without incident or casualty. And keep it all to himself. Forever."

"Like where? There's a few places I'd rather not revisit."

"I can assure you." Tauber's nervous smile returned. "That your assignment will not take you anywhere you have ever been to before."

The drive was dull and Dwayne dozed through most of it. Doc Tauber wanted to keep his mystery intact and he had little to say. Their route took them into the afternoon sun riding west out of Vegas on a two-lane as straight as a string in a Land Rover badly in need of an alignment. The two men had zero in common. They talked some about their hometowns and the weather in Nevada. They ran out of small talk and Dwayne wasn't much in the mood anyway. All he wanted to know about was the job, and Doc was turning it into theater. The doc tried to break the awkward silence by turning on the radio. NPR, of course. Dwayne was unconscious within thirty seconds.

It was desert dusk when a change in the road surface brought him awake. Three tours in Iraq and two in Afghanistan made Dwayne sensitive to things like that. He came around with a start. His hand clutched for the pistol grip of his rifle, but it wasn't there. They were climbing a rutted road that twisted up between rocks and scree. After a half-hour, he could see they were approaching a tall structure that rose spindly and black against the streaked sky of the orange sunset. The road leveled out. As they pulled closer on the rutted trail, Dwayne could see it was a steel tower structure holding a globe about sixty feet off the sand. The globe was polished sheet metal and looked about ten feet in diameter. The ball caught the final rays of the dying day and cast an oily sheen from its surface. From the center of the globe, a steel rod rose another thirty or forty feet. The rod was secured in place with guy wires all around. It was topped by a flashing strobe.

"Is that a lightning rod?" Dwayne asked.

"It's a Tesla tower," the doc replied. "Awesome, isn't it?"

"Looks like a ride at a state fair," Dwayne said.

Tauber laughed. Not a condescending chuckle at Dwayne's ignorance, but an open, honest laugh that surprised them both. Dwayne decided that he liked this geek.

The Land Rover pulled up to a trio of Quonset huts on the roof of a mesa. The collection of sand-blasted and sunbaked buildings were near the lip of the escarpment they'd been climbing up over the past thirty minutes. There was a dirt bike and a beat-to-shit Acura there. What looked like an old cargo container was partly buried in a high humpback dune beyond the Q-huts.

As Dwayne and the doc got out of the Rover, two guys stepped from one of the huts. They were short and dark. One was bearded and wore a Welcome to Reno t-shirt. The other was clean-shaven, except for a Saddam mustache. He wore an aloha shirt in a pineapple pattern. They studied the newcomers for a few seconds and went back inside without saying a word.

"That's Parviz and Quebat," Tauber said. "They're Iranian."

"They got a convenience store in there?" Dwayne said.

"No. They're nuclear physicists."

"Iranian nuclear physicists?"

"They stay here all the time," Tauber said. "They're kind of on a watch list. And they can't go home because they're homosexuals."

"That must be a tough beat," Dwayne said.

He followed Tauber as the doc trotted away toward the tower rising into the gloom.

"Nicola Tesla was a genius," the doc said. "Greater than Edison. A seer. He invented the idea of this tower over a hundred years ago with the intention of projecting broadcast energy via electromagnetism. Imagine a network of these across the country drawing power from the air and providing inexpensive energy to anyone. And all without a single wire."

"So, it's a lightning rod," said Dwayne. He began to wonder if this was a job or an investment pitch.

"In a way," the doc said and slapped the base of a steel leg. It created a soft thrumming sound in the guy wires leading away from the globe.

"A massive power surge is required to jumpstart it. The surge runs to steel rods driven a hundred and thirty feet into the rock below the tower. That creates a cone of electromagnetic energy around the globe that spreads across the entire compound."

"Uh huh," Dwayne said. He was checking the perimeter around them. Force of habit. The compound rested on the edge of a rocky mesa that dropped off to mile after mile of flat, featureless desert. In the dark, it looked like the land on the approach to Baghdad. Empty and quiet. The dark was closing in as the sun set quickly. The horizon would soon be invisible.

"That EMP lasts only seconds. But it's enough to power the Tauber Tube which is here," said the doc as he walked across the compound to the rusting cargo container. The opening and six feet at the front of the cargo box were exposed, but the remaining fifty feet or so was buried in a high pile of freshly dug sand.

There was a steel vent at the crest of the pile, and a thin trail of vapor escaped from it. An old Case backhoe sat on a trailer in some greasewood nearby.

There were two dirt bikes standing up under tarps by it. Tauber threw the door lever down and pulled at a hatch cover set at the end of the container. The squeal of the hinges echoed off the rocks all around. Doc grunted with the effort. Dwayne lent a hand, and the door swung wide. A gust of chilled air escaped from the dark interior.

"And this is what you want me to guard?" Dwayne asked.

"I didn't bring you out here to guard the Tube," the doc said. "I need you to go *through* the Tube."

"A time machine?" Dwayne asked.

"In its simplest terms?" Tauber said, "yes."

The half-buried cargo container served as an entryway to a block-walled chamber that was a thousand square feet minimum with a twenty-foot ceiling. Exposed vents poured cold air down into the room from above. This chamber was at the heart of the hill of fresh earth. There was a computer workstation set on a steel table. Doors to some rooms lined one wall. One door was open, and Dwayne could see a row of tiled stall showers. There were some pieces of equipment covered with cloths along another wall.

The farthest end of the big room was dominated by a row of thick, concentric coils with a corrugated steel platform suspended on the inside of the coils as a floor or walkway. There was enough clearance to allow a man to walk into the coil array without stooping.

The walkway led fifty feet to where the rank of coils ended at the rear wall of the big room. Vapor bled off the framework. They were rimed with some kind of ice or condensation. The whole coil array and walkway sat on a framework atop a poured concrete slab. The big room was a deep freeze after the desert heat. There was a chemical tang in the air.

"I walk through those Freon tubes, and I could meet Cleopatra?" Dwayne said.

"Conceivably," the doc replied. He was pleased that Dwayne was getting it.

"I rode all the way out here with you," Dwayne turned to him and spoke without inflection. "I may as well hear the rest."

"Without going into the physics or resorting to equations, the Tube creates a field that halts and then reverses the flow of time," Tauber said. "This requires a tremendous amount of power which we get by amping up the tower with a surge. That creates a mega-joule response from the tower, which increases the power of the initial jolt exponentially. There are limitations, of course. We can only crank up the necessary wattage once in a forty-eight hour period and then for only a thirty-minute window."

"You must get a hell of a bill from Nevada Electric," Dwayne said. He noticed his breath came out as vapor.

"Oh, we're off the grid completely," the doc said. "We can't have anyone asking questions. That's why we have a nuclear reactor."

"Where?"

"Inside one of the Q-huts. A generation four reactor. No waste. Totally shielded, very little spike in the background radiation. Just a small unit, really. Smaller than the one on a submarine."

"Run by your Iranian pals who are on a terror watch list," said Dwayne. He knew the first phone call he'd be making when he got back to Vegas.

"Yes. Parviz and Quebat are very proficient. Tehran's loss is our gain. The Tauber Tube would be impossible without their contribution."

"And you named this mother of all refrigerators after yourself?"

"Oh no," the doc said. "It's named for my sister Caroline. She made the calculations and developed the science that made time travel a possibility. My area is engineering, mainly."

"So, where's your sister, Doc?"

"She's somewhere out there," said Tauber. He gestured down the walkway into the coils.

"About one hundred thousand years ago."

———

Dwayne was seated in one of the Q-huts now with a Dos Equis tallboy in his fist. He hated Dos Equis. But it was ice cold and wet and the only brand in the house. The hut was drywalled inside with a carpeted floor and furnished with stuff from Walmart. Futon sofa, particleboard kitchen table, and lawn chairs. It reminded him of the dorm he lived in during his one semester at State before joining the army. All but the poster of a teenage Leonardo DiCaprio on the wall. That was a touch from the two Iranians who were in the next room. Sounds of Wii tennis came from within punctuated by laughter and curses in Persian.

Doc Tauber sat across the table from Dwayne and fidgeted.

"I know this is hard to grasp at first," Tauber began.

After a mouthful of beer, Dwayne raised a hand for silence. He swallowed.

"Your sister and two other guys—"

"—Dr. Miles Kemp and a grad student from UC Davis named Phillip," the doc said.

"They went into this coil for a trial run about a week ago, and they didn't come back," Dwayne said.

"We can open the field for thirty minutes once every forty-eight hours. We've done that three times since they went through and none of them have returned back through the Tube. Something has to have gone wrong on the other end."

"What's on the other end, Doc?"

"Nevada, as it was one hundred millennia ago. Where we are now would be on the shore of a shallow sea almost a thousand miles across. The geologic record for this period gives us a reasonable amount of certainty on that, for this exact location. You see, though the Tube allows travel through time it doesn't—"

"—take you through *space*," Dwayne said. "I saw the movie, Doc. And you want me to go through the Tube and rescue your sister."

"And Dr. Kemp and Phillip."

"Rescue them from what, Doc?"

"Well, the time period is teeming with dangerous lifeforms. Basically, giant versions of animals familiar to us today. Giant bear. Giant beaver. Giant moose. Even elephants at that period. There could also be violent storms or floods. It's impossible to know what conditions are on the other side without going through the Tube."

"People?"

"No indigenous people," Tauber said. "The oldest known human habitation is 60,000 years ago at the outside. And that's the Topper site on the Savannah River in South Carolina. We chose our target destination because of the total lack of Paleo-Indian habitation. You'd be outside that window."

"So." Dwayne set down the empty and popped another open. "I go back there and find out your sister and her pals were eaten by a giant squirrel. Or they went through and wound up at the bottom of the sea. Or inside a mountain. Or that they were just vaporized by your machine as soon as they stepped inside. And that could happen to me if I go on this snipe hunt."

"No!" said Tauber and stood up. "I had momentary contact with them on the other side. A signal, using the Tauber Wave

Generator Transmitter. Some clear transmissions ending in a garbled one. They arrived in prehistoric Nevada alive and intact."

"Tauber wave generator? Your sister's a busy gal," Dwayne said and took a long pull of the tallboy.

"The transmitter is my invention," the doc said.

Dwayne set the beer down and stood up. "Okay, take me back to my motel. Drive me back or I'll take the Rover myself in exchange for the time you wasted."

"You're walking away from three people in danger? You'll just let them die?"

"I'm supposed to believe this bullshit?"

"So, you're leaving?" Tauber said. His eyes were pleading, his lips a quivering line. "I was told you were suited for work like this. High risk. High reward."

"Did Mulroy mention that I'm not crazy? Or would you know the difference? I wouldn't stay for a million bucks, Doc," said Dwayne as he made for the door.

"What about ten million?"

Dwayne let the screen door swing closed. "We talking before or after taxes?" Dwayne said.

"We're talking cash. What you tell Uncle Sam is on your conscience."

"Break it down for me," Dwayne said. "The events leading up to the last time you saw them."

Tauber was nursing the same beer at the table in the kitchenette. A one-beer guy at most.

"It was just a trial run, or that's what it was *supposed* to be. Caroline, Phillip Worth, and Dr. Kemp would go first. They didn't carry much equipment other than the wave transmitter and some calibration gear. No recording devices or cameras. There were no weapons because they didn't expect that kind of encounter. They wore the same clothing I can supply you with: organic, decomposable materials that would leave no trace for archeologists should something go wrong."

"No prehistoric Izod labels, right?" Dwayne said.

"Right. We adjusted the power levels for the time period we wanted. The Tube takes forty-eight hours to create the desired field, which we can hold open for thirty minutes or less. The three of them walked down the tube, and within minutes, they were transmitting text back to me."

"What kind of messages?"

"Just that they had made it through the field safely and to confirm that they were in the target era."

"How could they know that, Doc?" said Dwayne.

"The plant life. The topography and, most accurately, the position of the stars."

"It was night when they arrived?"

"Sometime after midnight. August 11th, 104,987 BC. I calculated that with a program from Caltech using the position of Orion relayed through the transmissions. The last messages were about the climate and then a long period of silence. Just before the field closed, I received this text message. That's the last contact I had with them."

Tauber held up a sheet of hand-printed notes. The line at the bottom of the page read:

HNTGHRNS MST HDE

"What does it mean?" Dwayne said.

"I have no idea. It could be a panicked typo or someone's hand on the transmitter when they moved it."

"How many days ago was this?"

"Seven days. But for Caroline and the others, only a few hours will have passed if I can send a second team through. I thought of going myself, but I'm the only one who can run the programs for the Tube. If I went through, I would be dooming all of us to remaining in the past forever."

"What about your Iranian friends?" Dwayne asked. The sounds from the other room had turned from digital tennis to muffled exchanges of dialogue from a television. The boys were watching their shows.

"They're here only to maintain the reactor. They weren't part of the theory work. They have no real interest in the core goals we were working toward. This was a closely held project. Very secret. You can understand."

"You said you can open the field to just hours after their first arrival," Dwayne said. "Why not open it to before they get there?"

"There are reasons not to do this. Involved, hard-to-explain, dangerous reasons. But, trust me, attempting to overlap openings past our initial arrival point would be unbelievably bad."

"So, bottom line," Dwayne said. "What do you need from me?"

"I need you to go through the Tube, kick any ass you have to, and bring my sister back alive. And Phillip and Miles, of course."

"I might need some help to do that. Get me back to Vegas. I have some people to see."

"Would a cash advance help?" Tauber asked.

"That would go a long way, Doc."

2

CHAZ RALEIGH

The pull order said 2011 Cadillac. But it was an Escalade that sat in the driveway roundabout in front of the Florida-ugly mini-mansion. Tinted glass. Spinners. Vanity plate, G8TRS.

"I do not like Escalades," Chaz said with a sigh. He threw the clipboard up on the dash of the tow truck. Chaz was sitting shotgun.

Fat Paolo Diaz was driving and peered from the clipboard to the black SUV across the street.

"Most brothers dig Escalades," Paolo said. "Well, not this brother," Chaz said. "This black man has honor. That ride is for pimps and middle-aged real estate agents."

"Tags match the order. Don't see no club on her," he said. "She's a driveaway, not a tow."

"Escalade," Chaz said. "A car for agnostics. People who can't make up their mind. Do I want a pimpmobile or a whoopie war machine? Oh, I'll get *both*. An SUV all pussied up with wood-grain dash and seat warmers and more cupholders than a multiplex. Shit."

"Uh-huh," Paolo said. He yawned and covered his mouth with a chubby hand.

"And the house," Chaz said. "Bet this clown bought at the top of the market. Now he's underwater and can't make the nut. Car's in the drive 'cause the garage is full of the jet skis and a fan boat and all the other shit he bought with equity loans."

"You good, then?" Paolo said.

"Yeah. You shove off. Krispy Kreme ain't heard from you in an hour, and they're getting worried," Chaz said. He climbed out of the airconditioned cab into the wet Tampa heat with the paperwork and a master key in hand.

"Fuck you too," Paolo said and put the tow in gear and pulled away.

The key slid into the driver's door lock, and when Chaz turned it, something went *woop woop woop* under the hood and a recorded voice (it sounded like Lee Majors) said, "You are not authorized to enter this vehicle." The *woop*ing continued between cautious reminders from the bionic man as Chaz slid his weightlifter bulk behind the wheel. Tight fit. The owner must be a damn midget. And there was no adjusting the seat until the engine turned over. He couldn't even get the door closed and rested a Timberline on the chrome step rail.

He cranked the master key in the ignition, and the big eight roared to life. All the exterior lights went on all around the house. The front door blew open and a pit bull charged out growling low. A rail-skinny dude wrapped in a Sleeping Beauty beach towel and nothing else stormed onto the lawn. Nothing else? Does a 12-gauge pump count?

Chaz tromped the accelerator and reversed the Escalade through some hydrangeas, leaving parallel black patches on the green-painted driveway. The front windshield starred as he fought the wheel and did a Brody over the neighbor's sprinkler-slick lawn. Double-aught punched the suicide door glass in as Chaz got the luxury-priced beast straightened out and off the curb, snapping off a cast-iron mailbox post on his way. He settled down on the pavement and slammed the lever to D, but the pit bull was on the hood now, nails making squealing sounds on the finish as it fought to stay on board. The mailbox was caught under the trannie and throwing sparks behind the SUV all the way down the block.

The owner was in the street now, and the beach towel left behind on the lawn. Bare-butt naked, he emptied the shotgun at his own sweet candy-ass ride with a howl of fury. But Chaz was flying. The buckshot took off a rearview and sent some chrome trim flying. Finally, the car had some character.

The dog wasn't giving up though. It frantically scratched at the starred windshield until it collapsed the glass and followed a storm of crystalline beads right into Chaz's lap. Man and dog crammed in the close space. All Chaz knew was that he wanted to bail. Let the bank deal with this asshole and his asshole car and his asshole dog.

Out the door and rolling just like the jump instructor at Benning taught him. Hurt just as bad, too. He wound up flat on his chapped ass and watched the Escalade roll to the end of the block and into a pond.

Sirens. And the paperwork was in the car. This was no place for a black man in the middle of the night.

He trotted away down the street with the dog barking at him from its perch on the Escalade slowly sinking in the dark water.

He hiked to a Shell station off Linebaugh and called a Rainbow Cab to take him back to the garage. His cell phone was ringing the whole way, Suncoast Tow and Storage wanting to know where he was. They'd already heard from the sheriff. Maybe animal protection, game and wildlife, and the homeowners' association, too. He was sure of that. Chaz had a story. He just was too damned tired to tell it right now. At best he'd lose his job. At worst, his bond.

"Tell you what," Chaz told the Haitian driver. "Take me to Jalisco Pines instead."

A ten-minute ride in the opposite direction and he climbed out at his condo and paid the driver.

"You have glass in your face." A man, a big man, was stepping from the shadows under a clump of date palms as the cab pulled away. Chaz's hand moved toward the .38 snubby he kept in a clamshell holster in the waistband of his jeans under the muscle shirt.

"You're not gonna need that," Dwayne Roenbach said. "Not unless you're still sore over Manila."

"That bitch?" Chaz said and brought his hand out to grip Dwayne's arm. "Can't even remember her name."

"Sure, you do." Dwayne grinned.

In the kitchen, Chaz poured them both a few fingers of J&B. Dwayne looked around at the boxes piled against one wall and the TV sitting on the floor in front of a folding chair.

"I see you settled in," Dwayne said.

"Unless they were born here, everyone in Florida thinks they're leaving someday," Chaz said.

"How about tonight?"

"You got something up, bro?"

"Crazy money for a little job right here in the good old USA." Dwayne drained the jelly glass.

"What kind of time we talking about?" Chaz said.

"Well, as I've come to learn recently," Dwayne said. "Time is kind of relative."

3

JAMES "JIMBO" SMALL

The hide was broiling hot all day long. Now the sun was going down and the cold already setting in as the rocks bled their heat into the dark. Jimbo was set up under a shelf of rock below the crest of a hill with a Ghillie mat draped over him. The fat barrel of the Winchester 70 was wrapped in burlap to hide its shape.

Below him, a row of steel posts and drooping mesh topped with coils of razor wire were all that separated his hide in Arizona from a field of fire on the Mexican side. He pressed a sweaty brow to the 30x scope and the shitty little fence leaped into view. He could see the broad gully that was carved under a section of the fence by some long-ago washout. The footprints left by sneakered and sandaled and cowboy-booted feet were clearly imprinted in the dust at the floor of the gully. All going one way. All leading into the land of the Big Promise.

"International border my red ass," Jimbo said to himself.

But no action so far today. The tip called into the sheriff at the reservation wasn't playing out. Some mules carrying *mucho* bundles of primo shit up from Nogales were supposed to cross here and follow the deer trails north through the Pima reservation land. Hot lead, no lie.

No show either. But there was weather south of here earlier. He watched the dark clouds build on the horizon on the Mex side all afternoon. It might have held them up. He'd wait until full dark before calling it a day.

Jimbo slowly drew in the Winchester and put it aside. He skinned the nylon case off the Armalite. It was a sniper model with a NOD night vision scope in place atop it. He snapped open the bipod, wrapped it in burlap sacking and set it snug in place aimed down the hill toward the fence line.

The fence line jumped into sharp focus in a monochromatic view that made the scrub and scree look like the surface of the moon. He didn't want to look through the Starlite too long and lose his own natural night vision. Lots of guys he knew, *used* to know, got kakked because they were night-blind from staring into the scope for too long. Hadjis crept right up on their ass with them nearly sightless from long hours looking downrange in the artificial daylight, counting on their spotter to watch over them. Spotter goes down, and where are you? Blind as a newborn kitten.

Voices. Coming up to him from below. Not surprising. They crossed here all the time. No need to be quiet. He took a turkey-peek through the scope. No one in sight yet. They were down below his sightline, still on the Mex side.

He keyed the press button on his headset and spoke low.

"Deputy Small. Anyone there?" A crackle in his ear.

"What's up, Jimbo?" The drawl of Lester Horse.

"Got traffic down here heading my way."

"You have a visual, Jimbo?"

"I can hear 'em makin' for the fence line. You close, Lester?"

"Depends on where you are, Jimbo."

"I'm above that draw where the deer trail crosses near that spot where Dan Squires found the dirt bike last winter."

"Damn, Jimbo." Crackle and crosstalk. Jimbo could hear Lester talking to someone off- mike. Probably his partner John Haytown.

"Lester?"

"We're all the way the hell up on the east fire road near the highway fork. "

Jimbo took another turkey-peek. He could see them now. They were scrambling down the wall of the gully on the other side of the fence.

"They'll be over by the time you get here, Les."

"How many?"

"I count eight."

"Loaded down?"

Through the scope, they were closer now. Six were carrying bundles on their backs. Backpack suitcases packed with brown, flake, or most likely grass. Two, maybe three million dollars walking right toward him. The two who weren't humping rucks wore brand new cowboy hats and had rifles or shotguns shoulder-slung.

"Carryin' weight, Les. Six mules humpin' and two coyotes walkin' heavy."

More crackling and crosstalk. Busy night on the border.

Les came back on. "Let 'em go, Jimbo."

"They'll be up in the reservations. You'll never find 'em."

"Let 'em pass, Jimbo. No John Wayne shit, okay?"

"Yeah. Small out."

Jimbo'd have to lay here quiet and allow them to pass below him. If he moved now, he'd be inviting fire. They could all be armed as far as he knew. Might as well lay still and watch the late show. He pressed his eye to the scope. They were fifty yards south of the fence. Two of the mules were smaller than the others. From their gait, he knew they were women. They struggled with their burdens more than the others. The end of a long day. Twelve or more miles walking with maybe ten more ahead of them before the night was through.

One of the coyotes stopped and held up a hand. They were close enough that Jimbo could hear the sound of his voice if not the words. What was this dude up to? Why the sudden caution?

The coyotes stopped the procession. They made a pantomime of looking about them in the dark. What could they see? There's no way in hell they knew Jimbo was watching them. They turned now, rifles unlimbered, and motioned to the mules to sit on the floor of the gully. One of the mules hesitated and was dropped to the dust with the butt of a rifle.

Jimbo knew what was next. He'd found the evidence of it enough times. These poor bastards paid all they had to get over the border to a job with decent wages. They even agreed to carry shit as part of the fare. Now some of them were going to pay with their dignity. The coyotes had the power now, so close to the prize, to make these peons endure further hardship.

A coyote pulled one of the girls to her feet and yelled orders at her. He wanted that pack off her. When she struggled to shrug out of the straps, he pulled at her and, freeing her from the ruck, threw her to the ground. The other coyote held his rifle on the others and they sat, shifting in the sand until he shouted at them to be still.

The girl was young. Jimbo could tell that much. She tried to crawl up the lip of the shallow draw. The laughter rose up and echoed off the rocks, and Jimbo felt the flesh on his forearms go cold. The coyote was on top of the girl now, and they both slid down the wall of the draw and out of his sight. But he could hear the sounds. The pleading and the answering shouts. The other one stood with rifle trained on the mules and turned now and then to watch his amigo's progress with an eagerness that was plainly visible in his body language. He was doing the horny dance in his shiny rodeo boots while waiting for his shot at sloppy seconds.

Jimbo could easily move now—slide from his position while they were occupied. Take his gear and move up to where his ATV was hidden under a desert camo tarp. No one would blame him. No one had to know. They were on *their* side of the line, for Christ's sake.

Fuck it. Just fuck it.

He leaned into the scope again. He willed his shoulders to unbunch, his hands to unclench. He spat out the smooth round pebble he'd been sucking on and breathed in a clean lungful of cold air. Blew it out slow enough it wouldn't ruffle a butterfly's wings. When his lungs were empty, he settled the triple hairs on the head of the sucker standing and waiting his turn.

Center shot. It was a heavy round Jimbo custom loaded himself in his garage shop. It threw the guy from his field of vision. He moved the scope to the lip of the draw where he last saw Coyote One drop out of sight.

Like a prairie dog, the fucker popped up his head to look around in animal panic. The soft lead took him square in the neck. Cut short in mid-shout. A sweep of the scope found the coyote who'd been waiting for sloppy seconds face down and still in the dust with a dark shadow spreading under him.

The mules were running wild away into the dark, their bundles forgotten. They'd be back to cross the fence some other night. But not tonight. He brought the scope back to the lip of the draw in time to see the girl rise into his field of vision. She was pulling her clothes tight around her and looked about her with wide eyes that flashed white in the scope's harsh contrast. She bent to pick up one of the rifles and held it in her hands uncertainly.

Jimbo was unable to turn away as she brought the butt of the rifle down again and again on the skull of her attacker. Big over-head swings until she could no longer lift her arms. She stood exhausted and heaving and dropped the rifle to the ground.

"Come on, *bonita*," Jimbo said under his breath.

The girl looked toward Mexico *lindo* and home and turned back to gaze straight into Jimbo's eyes. Then she crawled on her belly under the fence and ran down the draw, heading north toward the golden lights of America.

"Good girl," he said to himself and stayed put for an hour before snaking out of his hide.

He sat in Josie's Fuel-and-Food on the highway, lingering over a second coffee and a third Marlboro. It was noon, and he wasn't on shift for a few more hours. Jimbo reviewed the night before. Dropping those Mexes. Watching the girl crawl under the fence. Hell, she probably already had a job in Tucson. Making beds at a Best Western or cleaning stalls at a horse barn.

He thought about how he belly crawled under that fence with his entrenching tool and buried those two *hombres* in a single grave away from the draw. Took near to dawn. He left the bundles of dope where the mules left them. Somebody'd come pick them up. Waste not, want not.

In a couple of hours, he'd be asked to fill out a report. He'd make up some politely-worded lies about the night before. An incident report with no incidents. He'd wallpaper over two murders like they never happened. It was bullshit piled on more bullshit. He'd be lying if he said he felt sorry for those *cabrones*. He'd be lying if he said he wouldn't do it all over again. Two assholes the world would never miss but they were dead and buried, and he killed them and dug their graves. And that was in his rearview no matter what and it would prey on him.

That's what his life was now. Pretending to enforce laws that his betters didn't have the *cojones* to stand by. Those fuckers could rape young girls and murder their mules and bring that shit across the border every night and make the tribe's land their goddamn golden highway, and Jimbo wasn't even allowed to ask them their business or even their names without getting himself in a world of shit. He smeared out the Marlboro and scooted the coffee mug across the Formica.

"Well, what put you on the warpath, chief?" said someone standing over the booth.

Jimbo half-rose, a fist white-knuckled and drawing back.

Dwayne Roenbach stood grinning at him.

Jimbo's face creased in a smile that almost hurt. The two men embraced. Regulars at Josie's looked up to see the unusual sight of Deputy James Small hugging another man, and the even more unusual spectacle of the dour Pima lawman looking happy.

Dwayne shoved Jimbo away.

"You got anything tying you down, Small?" Dwayne said. "A woman? Family?"

"Nothin' I can't walk out on," Jimbo said.

"That badge?"

"Don't mean shit," Jimbo said. "Not to me. Not to nobody else neither."

4

RICK RENZI

The house was probably nice once. Three bedrooms, two baths, two-car garage, a little split level on a decent lot in a nice enough subdivision outside Cincinnati. But the lawn had gone to hell, the siding was grungy, and the paint around the windows was peeling away.

Dwayne and Chaz climbed out of the rental car and made their way up the cracked walk.

"I'm already sorry I came along for the ride," Chaz said.

"The hell you are," Dwayne said. "You'd push your own sister down a well to get on that corporate jet."

"You figure out who's payin' the bills yet?"

"Jimbo's working on that. He's been running it down on his laptop. So far he's just finding a bunch of shell corporations."

"At least it ain't government," Chaz said. Dwayne pressed the doorbell and heard a pleasant three-chord chime echoed within the house. He rang again and heard a thump and a crash of glass. The door opened a crack, and a wiry-looking man in a stained t-shirt and wrinkled running pants glared at them from painfully red eyes.

"You didn't answer your phone, Renzi," Dwayne said.

"Thought you were the pizza guy," Rick said. His voice was a croak. His breath was foul with tobacco and whatever he'd been drinking. His body gave off the rich stink of weeks of neglect. An ashtray smell with an aftertaste of rotting food was seeping out of the house.

"You gonna let us in?" Chaz said.

In answer to that the door slammed.

"We came all the way here, right?" Dwayne said. Chaz nodded.

A double shoulder hit took the door off its hinges and carried the two big men into the middle of the living room.

Renzi didn't even get up from the sofa.

"I'm not sharing the pizza when it gets here," he said. He popped the top on a fresh beer and took a long pull.

The sofa was the only piece of furniture in the room. There was an open trash bag in a corner spilling empties of Yuengling quarts and cans to the carpet. Empty pizza boxes were in an untidy pile along one wall, forming a cardboard condo development for a swarm of roaches. An open pizza box on the coffee table was an impromptu ashtray piled with butts. There were chips in the plaster where pictures once hung. Pictures of Rick's family. Wife and three kids.

"Nothing nastier than a beer drunk," Chaz said. He sniffed the air.

"When did she leave?" Dwayne said.

"A month," Renzi said and slouched back, resting the can on his knee.

"You got *this* fucked up in a month?" Chaz said.

"We have a job," Dwayne said. "Short-term, with a big payday. You could get them back."

"Had a job," Renzi said with a snort. "Had a lot of jobs. Got pissed on or pissed off. Whatever you got goin', I'd just shit all over it."

"I need you for the one thing you do right," Dwayne said. "Blowing shit up."

30

"Forget it," Renzi said. "Nothing you say is gonna get me off this couch. Nothing you do is gonna get me out of this house. I'm past whatever it is you want me for. I'm used up. I'm tired. Find someone else."

The fight was a short one. Renzi was too long drunk and too long tired. They tossed him into the back of the rental and drove away from the sad little split-level.

"Wish we threw him in the shower first," Chaz said and rolled down the windows.

Renzi's head hurt in a new way. A couple of new ways. The old hangover pain behind his eyes and on top of his head was there. But his right cheek was sore, too. The inside of his mouth was cut. And his left ear hurt.

"Drink this, Ricky." Dwayne was offering a glass tinkling with ice.

Renzi sat up. He was in a broad swivel chair covered in plush leather. He accepted the tumbler and looked around. He was in a long narrow room with upholstered walls, a paneled bar and a big screen TV with a golf game on it. He took a sip. It was ice water.

"Drink it," Dwayne said. "It'll clear your ears."

"Ears?"

"You're on a plane, dumbass," Chaz said and switched the TV to a poker show.

"We're going to Nevada," Dwayne explained. "That's where the job is."

"You guys steal this jet?" Renzi asked.

"Belongs to our client," Dwayne said. "We still don't know who that is. But they've paid all our expenses and a solid advance against a ten million dollar payout. Tax-free cash. The job is a

31

week, maybe. Most of that is prep time. The actual mission is one or two days tops, and it's domestic."

"Something legal?" Renzi said. "You guys don't expect me to blow a safe or like that?"

"Nothing illegal," Dwayne said. "But it's a corporate secret. No talking about it after."

"Like Tikrit," Renzi said. "Just like that," Chaz said.

"Is Hammond in on it?" Renzi said.

"No," Dwayne said. "This is my deal. I don't even know where in the world Hammond is."

"I hear he's back in the States," Renzi said. "I heard that, too," Chaz said.

"Hammond's not part of this," Dwayne cut in. "It's not his kind of play."

"Okay, I'll come along and look it over." Renzi sat back.

"Like you have a choice," Chaz said.

"Hey." Renzi gestured toward the bar with his glass. "Any chance I can get a little drink?"

"No way," Dwayne said. "You have forty-eight hours to straighten your ass up before I let you anywhere near det cord and Semtex."

5

THE RUNDOWN

The following morning, the four men gathered in the largest Q-hut, which would serve as an operations center for the mission. The biggest room within was soundproofed and windowless and held computer workstations with big flat-screen monitors. These monitors swam with a screensaver image of rolling surf.

"Everything must be done to reduce your impact on the environment," Dr. Tauber said. "Your clothing, body armor, and footwear are made from chemical-free paper and vegetable-based materials so they decompose rapidly."

"This some Al Gore bullshit?" Renzi said. "That means no smokes either, Ricky," Chaz said.

Dwayne stepped in. "Think of it more like a covert necessity. We have to get in and get out, and no one can ever know we were there. Ever. If something goes wrong and we don't get back, there can't be any evidence we were there. Imagine someone digging around in the desert, and they find a hundred-thousand-year-old Swiss Army knife where it has no business being. It may seem like a long time ago, but the doc tells me that you'd be surprised at the stuff that survives to be found."

"So we pick up our brass," Jimbo said.

"No brass," Dwayne said. He reached into one of the large steel equipment crates that were stacked along one wall. "We'll be armed with these."

Dwayne held up an ugly black rifle about two feet in length, a bullpup design with a heavy box magazine mounted near the rear of the weapon. The three ex-Rangers studied it with something like hunger. Whatever this new piece was, it was these weapons that would help them stand up to any threat they met. It would be the difference between dying and getting back alive. He tossed the rifle to Jimbo.

"We have ten of these. They fire a .30 caliber rocket round propelled by a mix of two chemicals ignited electrically from a battery worn on our belts. Twenty-round magazines. The rounds are frangible and made of compressed organic matter. Hard enough to penetrate any living target but composed of materials that will degrade—break down—over time. The frame is steel and ceramic and will biodegrade within a thousand years."

"Who built these?" Jimbo said.

"I used Vinnie Barnes in Tulsa," Dwayne said. "He's expensive, but he's good. They're based off a design of his he's been working on for a while. And he doesn't ask questions or kiss and tell."

"You tried one of these on a range, Dwayne?" Jimbo inspected the rifle.

"It's accurate enough within fifty yards, and jamming is minimal," Dwayne said. "It's lots quieter than any piece we're used to. But the punch it offers is considerable. There's two charges in each projectile. The first forces the projectile from the barrel at less than ballistic speed. A second charge goes off once it's in free air and traveling downrange. That brings the speed to three-K FPS. That means the muzzle energy increases exponentially as it nears the target. We won't be up against a military, or even a human, opponent so we don't need much range. But we do need punch. The missiles are a mix of explosives and slugs. Chances are we won't need these at all. And if we do it'll be against wildlife that will most likely run the first time we fire at them. But you're our gunhound, Jimbo. I want your opinion on this pig."

"Will do," Jimbo said. He was already stripping down the one in his hands.

"How about explosives?" Renzi said.

"Doc thinks Semtex won't be a problem," Dwayne said. "If we have to use it, it means it's been detonated. Any chemical traces that survive are likely to be negligible. Think you could work up some quick and dirty grenades for us?"

"Satchel charges do?" Renzi said. "They're easy to make and use."

"As long as it goes boom, bro," Dwayne replied, "make up a dozen."

"You have pictures of who we'll be looking for?" Chaz said to Dr. Tauber.

"They shouldn't be hard to find," Tauber said. "They'll be the only three humans on the continent. It won't be a matter of picking them out of a crowd."

"Just wanted to put faces to the names," Chaz said. "See who's who."

"I'm kind of curious, too," Dwayne said.

Tauber pulled up a photo file on one of the monitors.

"These are the most recent photos," Tauber said. "I can print some up." He began scrolling through the file, and there were shots of Doc Tauber with two other men. One was a heavyset man in his forties. Balding with the kind of thick beard some balding guys grow to compensate. It had to be Kemp. The other man was rangy and thin and in his twenties. Longish hair, goatee. Phillip Worth, the graduate student. They were happy in the photos. Dressed in outdoor wear and obviously on some kind of short hike. Phillip wore a Batman t-shirt.

"We took these on one of our excursions to scout out the

ground the team would be traveling over," Tauber said. The others stood close behind him. "The plant life and water table would be different at the destination. But the topography would be basically the same as it is now."

More pictures of the three men in and around the facility.

"Where's your sister?" Dwayne said.

"She took most of the photos," Tauber said.

He moved the mouse and opened another file.

A series of images showing a woman of about twenty-five who looked even younger when she smiled. The smiles were rare, though. Mostly candid shots of her intently studying monitors in the room they now stood in or making adjustments to their gear. Her posture betrayed a serious demeanor. Not the fussy type, her shoulder-length blonde hair pulled back in a simple ponytail. But in one shot the camera caught her unawares. It was from the earlier series of shots from the hiking expedition. A hand holding a beer and an arm thrown up to shade her face. An embarrassed smile or caught in mid-laugh. A band of zinc on her nose barely concealing a field of light freckles.

"Let's get to work," Dwayne said.

HNTGHRNS MST HDE

"This is it?" Chaz said. "You call this intel?"

"That's the text message my sister sent back through the wave transmitter," Dr. Tauber said. "It followed after a message telling me the local temperature and conditions. Then the transmissions stopped."

It was the night before the step-off date they all agreed on. The reactor was heating up and could provide the jolt the Tube needed by early the next morning.

The rocket guns had all been tested, stripped, and cleaned. They tried out one of Renzi's hemp-bag, eco-friendly satchel charges. It created enough shock and awe to satisfy all of them. They packed power bars in soy-based edible wrapping, leather *botas* for water, and a small medical kit with no plastic and a minimum of metal parts. They wouldn't need any radios as the unit was small and would stay tight. They'd take a wave transmitter with them. Doc worked another one up for them. They could send voice and texts back as long as the field was open. It had a record and re-send feature as well.

They were chowing down on pizza and beer and cooling out before the Big Day around a fire Jimbo laid in the desert beyond the huts.

"The first word is gibberish," Dwayne said. "I'm guessing the second phrase is 'must hide.' Hide from what?"

"We go find where they're hiding," Renzi said.

"I don't think it's going to be that easy," Dwayne said. "If hiding got them out of their trouble they'd have come back through the tube already when the field re-opened. They missed three opportunities. At the very least they would have sent another message. They're either in deep shit somehow or cut off from the field area."

"Or dead," Renzi said. Dwayne shot Renzi a look.

"So, Doc, what's the point of this whole thing?" Chaz said.

"I'm not sure I understand," said Tauber after a moment.

"The time machine," Chaz said. "You gonna hunt dinosaurs, rob a pharaoh's tomb, take a peek at Jesus, or what?"

"It's purely a scientific endeavor," Tauber said. "Frankly, Caroline, Dr. Kemp, and I weren't thinking much past the math. We were focused on proving the theory and building the Tube. We chose the first destination era because it was similar enough to present conditions with no risk of encountering any human population or catastrophic conditions."

"What's the money man's interest in your Tube?" Chaz asked. "He's laying down some serious cash here. I started with the ownership papers on that G-5 we flew in on but ran into a jungle of shell corps. A few of them had heavy ties with the feds."

"He's a man with a keen interest in physics and the advancement of knowledge."

"And some shady connections," Jimbo said. "Those two Axis of Evil escapees you have running the reactor. You didn't find them through any want ad."

"Our benefactor is a man of considerable influence," Tauber said. He seemed anxious to change the subject but knew they'd want something from him. "But I'd be violating a stack of non-disclosure agreements this high if I told you any more. Your fee for this mission buys him his privacy."

"You're right, Doc." Jimbo crushed a Coors can between his palms. "A quarter share of ten mill buys a shitload of shut-my-mouth."

"I still don't see a profit motive here," Chaz said. "That's an ass-load of cash to throw away just for curiosity. What's the practical purpose of time travel?"

"What was the practical purpose of going to the moon, dumbass?" Renzi said.

"They don't really share that kind of information with me," Tauber said. "For Caroline, Martin Kemp and I, the success of the Tauber Tube can lead us to practical experimentation to prove string theory. Have you heard of that?"

"I've heard of it," Chaz said. "Stephen Hawking, right?"

"Yes," said Tauber, who tried to cover his surprise.

"We read more than *Hustler* and weapons manuals, Doc," Dwayne said dryly.

"Uh-huh." Tauber blushed. "String theory posits that there are universes next to ours, similar but differing in subtle details to radical shifts in reality. It's long been theorized that these universes are created by disruptions in time rather than space. It's where history branches off in a new direction at a critical point."

"Like the South winning the Civil War," Chaz offered. "Or JFK surviving the assassination."

"Or the Lions winning a Superbowl," Renzi said and brayed.

"We are talking probabilities not fantasy," Tauber said.

It was the Rangers' turn to be surprised. The doc made a funny.

"So, if you go back to the past and fart around on purpose," Chaz said. "Won't you risk changing the present?"

"We've considered that and planned to devise some low impact tests that we could then return to the past to undo," Tauber said.

"Like what?" Dwayne wanted to know. "Well, we hadn't gotten that far in actuality," Tauber said with a dour expression. "And I hope we haven't already strayed into a temporal anomaly."

"Hey, where *are* Pervert and Queerbait?" Renzi said. He glanced over the hut. "I haven't seen them around."

"Parviz and Quebat went to Las Vegas for the day," Tauber said. "The reactor is entirely self-maintaining. But they'll be back in plenty of time to monitor the readings."

"They gamblers?" Renzi said.

"Celine Dion fans."

Dwayne stood on a ledge of shale and looked out over the moonlit desert. The temperature had dropped forty degrees since the sun went down. If the trail left by the three eggheads led that way, they'd be walking down this slope the following day and into the bowl-shaped depression below. It wouldn't look exactly like this if Tauber was right. It could be wooded or grassland. Somewhere below would be a lake, a marsh, or even an inland sea where there was now sand, rock, and dust. The doc assured the team that rocks don't lie.

Dwayne turned at the crunch of a boot heel. Chaz was climbing the natural steps up to him. Chaz clutched two beers, the necks between his fingers.

Chaz handed a bottle to Dwayne, and they stood looking over the desert.

"The Iranians are back," Chaz said. He took a pull off the Coors.

"They enjoy the show?" Dwayne said.

"They didn't share. They were wearing matching Celine t-shirts, though. You know they're not a couple?"

"Huh?"

"Parviz and Quebat. They're gay, but they're not each other's type."

"Good to know." Dwayne tipped the beer back in one long swallow.

"They're our ticket back, man," Chaz said. "I thought I'd talk to them. So we're not just strangers."

"Like when you always made sure the Black Hawk pilots knew all our names."

Chaz threw his empty far out into the dark.

A brittle pop echoed over the rocks.

"Renzi seems to be dealing," Chaz said after a moment. "He's sober. Cranky about having no smokes, though."

"He's good as long as he has someone to shoot at or blow up," Dwayne said. "It's the home side of it he sucks at. Jimbo's a smoker too, and he's not bitching."

"Ricky thinks he's going to get the wife and kids back."

"Never going to happen. Even if it does, if she comes back, he'd find a way to screw it up. And she'd only come back for the cash. I don't know her, so I don't know if she's that kind."

"Rick says she's a bitch."

"What else is he going to say?"

A coyote yipped somewhere out in the dark. "You think this is for real?" Chaz said.

"Going backward in time?"

"The money is," Dwayne said.

"Yeah. But all this science fiction bullshit."

"Doesn't matter. It's a payday. What do you believe?"

"I hope it's bullshit. I hope it's all smoke and mirrors and

Tauber's crazy and invented this story and all his machine does is keep beer cold. Because if all this is for real? We're walking into God knows what with our eyes shut."

"Quick in and out, bro. No unfriendlies."

"You can't know that. Our intel is non-existent. We know jack squat of what to expect on the other side."

"When's intel ever been one hundred percent? But this is hindsight, bro. We're going back into history, not a mystery." Dwayne threw his own bottle. It landed soundlessly somewhere out on the sand. "When *haven't* we been told one thing and got dropped into the middle of something we weren't expecting?"

"Yeah, but there was five of us then."

"Four's enough."

"Did you even call him, Dwayne?"

"I thought four was enough."

"I know it ain't the money because there's more than enough of that here."

"We don't need Hammond," Dwayne said.

"You might not say that on the other side."

"We needed him in Tikrit. We needed him in Kandahar and Quito. Remember when it all went south in Golol?"

"This is different."

"I don't see how."

"It's a rescue, not a raid. Hammond brings a whole lot of shit with him I'd rather not deal with. I don't need the variables. I have enough to think about."

"I damned sure hope you're right, bro," Chaz said. He turned and made his way down from the ledge back to the compound.

Dwayne stood studying the terrain for a moment. He tried to picture it as it would appear tomorrow. How it would be different and how much it would be the same all that way in the past. He decided that was a waste of time and followed Chaz back toward the lights below.

Together they neared the Q-huts. They saw someone out in

the dark near the tower. It was Tauber. He was pacing back and forth, holding a satellite phone to his ear. He waved at them as a greeting and a gesture that he was occupied and would speak to them soon.

"History, not a mystery," Chaz muttered, and they headed for their bunks.

Renzi was still up and seated at the kitchen table in the residence hut. He was sipping coffee and watching the tiny TV there with the volume all the way down. His eyes were on the silent screen where cars went round and round a track without seeing any of it.

Dwayne and Chaz got that "not in the mood" vibe and just said their goodnights and went to their bunks. Renzi grunted back.

He was still up with the TV on when Parviz and Quebat returned and bustled into the hut, chattering in Persian. They fell silent when they saw Renzi seated in the blue glow of the TV.

"Good show?" Renzi said.

"Oh, yes." Parviz smiled. "We've seen her a dozen times or more." He turned to Quebat and spoke in a hushed tone. Quebat fished in a plastic shopping bag and held up a t-shirt with an image of Celine at the mike large on the front. He turned it to show Renzi the legend on the back.

"*My Heart Will Go On,*" Renzi read out loud, "my little girl likes that song."

"Maybe we can get her a shirt for her," Parviz said. "Next time we go. After you and the others come back."

"Yeah, that'd be cool," Renzi said. "Or maybe I'll take her myself. I'll be able to afford it after this."

Both Iranians smiled the smiles they wore when they felt they did not quite understand what was being said to them. They excused themselves and left Renzi in the dark.

Morris Tauber stood outside huddled in a parka and listened to the voice on the other end of the sat phone. He nodded impatiently. Each time the voice paused, Tauber interjected with pleas and assurances. The voice broke in on him, and he paced as he listened. Then silence. Tauber wanted to throw the phone as far into the dark as his strength would allow. But it was his lifeline, and his sister's lifeline. He would need that connection to beg for more money, more time.

The compound came to life the following morning.

The four men stripped down and dropped their clothing, watches, wallets, and other personal items into tubs marked with their names in black Sharpie.

Tauber stood by to assist. He wore a neutral expression and kept his eyes on their faces. But his gaze could not help but stray to bodies marked with scars and garish tattoos. All four had some variation of the Army Rangers unit symbol on their arms: a grinning skull with crossed combat knives behind it. Rick Renzi had an impressive one on his back that covered his entire right shoulder. The skull wore sunglasses and a fatigue cap with a cigarette butt clutched in tombstone teeth. Crossed M-16s and We All Come Back were emblazoned in a scroll beneath. There were also the puckered scars from bullet wounds on each man. Chaz had a broad patch of skin on one thigh covered in pink flesh left speckled by shrapnel. Dwayne had some grafting on the left side of his belly, the skin slick and hairless. Each man had the kind of rough-worn bodies a soldier gets in the field. No prison muscle or sculpted flesh from a gym. These were bodies built by long marches laden with heavy packs, used hard by battle.

The men showered with a strong antibiotic, exfoliating soap as Tauber directed. It was part of the protocol for entering the Tube. They had to remove as much bacteria from their skin as they could. The theory was that many of the bugs living on them would be unwelcome strangers in Nevada 100,000 BC.

The Tube was prepared to power up. The coils were rimed with a thick coat of white ice and dripped clumps of wet, frozen nitrogen. A frigid mist spread from the tubes across the concrete floor of the big room. The interior temperature hung down around thirty degrees.

The monitors at the computer station were filled with graphs of floating bars, levels climbing and falling in tiny increments. Tauber turned to them now and again to make sure the levels were constant. He was up all night going over the programs to calibrate the window into which the field would open on the other side. He wanted the men emerging as close behind Caroline and the others as he could manage. That intense work kept him from reviewing and re-reviewing the phone conversation from the night before and what he might have said to make his case stronger.

The Rangers stepped shivering from the showers and lined up at the tables where their uniforms and underwear lay folded. The clothing was neutral colored and stiff.

Next came the ammo packs and gloves that were made from a thicker weave of the same paper-based cloth as their uniforms. Each man would carry ten clips for two hundred rounds total in addition to one of Renzi's special satchel charges. Two one-quart leather *botas* were worn on straps about their shoulders. Leather boots with leather soles held together with organic, decomposable glue. All was topped off with broad-brimmed boonie hats made of the crinkled paper cloth.

"We look like angry UPS drivers," Jimbo said.

"More like angry UPS *packages*," Renzi said. "These outfits make noise, man." The fabric was coarse and made a shushing noise when they walked.

"Don't start bitching this soon," Chaz said. "We don't need camo in the AO."

"Oh, I haven't *started* bitching, brother."

"You ain't my brother, Renzi. My brother's black."

It was all just grab-ass. Relieving the tension. Shaking out the kinks.

Guns were next. Each man picked up the rocket gun that they'd used on the range and zeroed in. Jimbo Small wrapped the fore-end of his weapon in strips of paper cloth he tore from one of the extra shirts.

"Cuts down on glare," he said. "Still say we could use a long-range gun."

"Barnes didn't work up any workable scopes," Dwayne said.

"These rocket rounds would have a wicked bad trajectory anyhow," Jimbo said. He shrugged and shouldered the weapon.

"Yeah," Dwayne said.

Tauber handed Dwayne what looked like a simple hand-held transmitter, a speaker with a built-in mike. A press key on the side was the only audio control. It had a retractable whip antenna, plus a foldout mini-keyboard for text.

"I built a new wave transmitter," Tauber said. "Easy to use. I modified it to carry audio. Just press to talk. It's made of soy-based plastic. Twenty-four-hour battery life. Just give me an initial check when you arrive and location updates as you make progress. Turn it off when not in use. It has a three-hour digital record feature and will turn the unit on and repeat your last broadcast every ten minutes. If the field's not open when you send I'll catch the replay."

"What's the range?" Dwayne asked. "Well…" Tauber said.

"Yeah, I know. You never got to test that," Dwayne said. He stuck the transmitter into a pocket on the leg of his pants.

Tauber produced a box and held it out to the group.

"Biodegradable wristwatches," he said. "Made of compostable paper. Good for about thirty days. You can keep me apprised of the relative time, so I can make my adjustments when I re-open the field in forty-eight hours."

The watches were digital with a flat face on a broad band colored in stripes of green and tan. "Set them at zero," Dwayne said as each man took a band.

The men stood strapping on the watches, adjusting packs and triple-checking the loads in their weapons and helping one another attach the line from each rifle to a belt-mounted battery pack.

"We're ready, Doc," Dwayne said and turned to the others. "Let's take a walk."

6

THE MISSION

A hot wind trilled through the guy wires of the steel tower as the noon sun beat down from a yellow sky. Low vibrations boomed from within the Q-hut that housed the reactor. Around the tower, the air filled with a frisson of static energy as a massive jolt of electricity ran from the reactor house, through shielded underground cables, to the pylons driven deep into the rock at the tower's base. The air was alive, bristling with anticipation.

A million wriggling serpents of bluish light engulfed the shining ball atop the tower. Thick arcs of pure electromagnetic power reached for the ground and turned the sand to thin puddles of glass wherever they made contact. There was an audible hiss as molecules collided and superheated air rushed to fill the vacuum left by the discharge. Man-made thunder shook the ground for miles around. A sheet of brilliance that would be mistaken for heat lightning could be seen as far away as Tonopah.

Inside the largest Q-hut, Parviz and Quebat sat at consoles in their lead-walled, rubber-floored control room and adjusted the flow of rapidly multiplying power into the Tube chamber. They wore disposable Tyvek bunny suits and thick goggles. The flatscreen monitors before them showed bar graphs spiking into the red. Other screens showed temperature, wattage, amperes, and reactor function. All wavering but within acceptable performance ranges.

Parviz spoke into a mike to the image of Dr. Tauber on one of his monitors. The image on the monitor was degraded by the free-floating power surge that engulfed the compound. It wavered but held firm enough for them to communicate.

"You have power, Doctor," he said in his Oxford-accented English.

In the Tube chamber, the four ex-Rangers stood in single file at the bottom of the steel ramp that led into the tunnel of frozen coils. The vapor from the concentric rings was growing thicker. The steel ramp, walkway, and railings were coated with a layer of slush that dripped from the thrumming coils.

Tauber called to the men from the computer station. "I can hold the field for thirty minutes. If you don't accomplish your mission in that time frame, you can either return or wait until I can re-open the field."

"How close are we going to come to your sister's team's arrival?" Dwayne called back. He blew into his gloved hands. Damn, it was cold.

"Hard to say," Tauber said. "I have to adjust the flow to the coils with the help of a modulation program. I'll try to get you there within an hour of their arrival. But it could be as much as a day. I just can't say."

"Sounds more and more like a goat-fuck all the time," Renzi said.

"Fire it up, Doc," Dwayne said.

"It's ready now," Tauber announced. "Anytime, gentlemen."

Dwayne led them down the walkway into a dense fog of frozen air. Each man followed, his footing uncertain on the slick steel grate.

Renzi was second. Then Smalls.

Chaz brought up the rear. And then they were gone.

Dwayne was on his hands and knees and bringing up everything he'd eaten that morning and the night before. He was wracked with chills and burning up all at the same time. His vision swam white and red. His mouth tasted like tin. There was a hammering pain inside the back of his skull.

He straightened up with eyes squeezed shut and shook his head from side to side. Still on his knees, he looked around for the others. They were each in varying stages of his own condition. Jimbo was bent over hawking up a stinking mess of bacon and oatmeal into the grass. Chaz stood bent, hands on knees and blowing out air in sharp exhales. There was puke all down the front of his brand new paper BDUs. Renzi lay on his back, making groaning noises and hissing through his clenched teeth.

Dwayne stood on shaking legs, and the pain in his head began to fade away. His stomach settled, and the chills abated. He spat out a mouthful of bitter juice. He turned to look back the way they came. There was a cloud of cold mist clinging to the ground. The field was still open. For now.

It was late afternoon. Around four o'clock by Dwayne's expert judgment of the bright yellow sun hanging in the west. He pressed his eyes shut once more and stood up straight for a look around.

They were roughly twenty feet beyond where the back wall of the Q-hut would stand a hundred thousand years from now. The mesa was still here and some of the same rock formations but there the similarity ended.

The slope up to the top of the mesa was now a long hill of loose rock scree sparsely covered in scrub pines gently moving in the breeze. It led down to a tree line with dense forest beyond. The trees thinned out as they reached the plateau top and the foliage changed to a thick wild grass studded with rock and stands of greasewood. The air was different, too. Thicker than the desert air. More humid. As he shook off the chill, Dwayne could feel the change in the air. It was rich with the smell of pine. Slightly cooler, too.

The only sign of animal life was the biggest damned butterflies Dwayne had ever seen, bright yellow and dappled with red. They drifted from one feathery seed pod to another atop the tall grass stalks. Each was fully the size of Dwayne's outstretched hand.

"That was a bitch!" Renzi said. He sat up and shoved his boonie hat back in place.

"Doc didn't say nothing about that crazy shit," Chaz said. He was stripping off gear harness to remove the vomit-foul tunic. He wore a paper fiber t-shirt underneath.

"He didn't know," Dwayne said. "There's no after-action report from the first trip through the Tube. That's why we're here, remember? You can complain when we get back."

"Maybe the trip killed them," Jimbo suggested.

Dwayne ignored that and stepped to the lip of an outcropping of shale. From the end of the rocky shelf, he looked down the slope to see a lake where the desert once was. Desert *will* be, he reminded himself. A spike of fresh pain behind his eyes. The lake was more like a sea or an inlet. It stretched away as far as he could see with broad beaches along its edge on either shore. It looked like low tide. Or maybe the water was receding, already turning to the bone dry bed it would be back in The Now.

The pine forest started about five hundred yards below them and covered a long slope right down to the water. Maybe two miles to the water. He couldn't see a beach directly below their position. Maybe there wasn't one, or maybe he just couldn't see it from this angle. Maybe the woods ended in marshes. It narrowed the search area. Caroline, Kemp, and Phillip had to be between here and the water somewhere. Unless they went the other way toward higher ground. He knew enough about tracking to know that people in unknown territory tended to walk downhill.

Dwayne spat some more of the bile taste out of his mouth and dug out the transmitter. He pressed the send button.

"Roenbach to Tauber. Mission time zero plus five. We're here, and it looks like the target area as you described it."

"Tell him this ride sucks," Renzi said. "Jimbo, can you pick up a trail?" Dwayne said. "Any sign?"

Jimbo wiped his mouth with the back of his hand and began to search the ground ahead. He waved a hand for the rest to stay where they were. Dwayne stepped off the shale to stand by Chaz. Renzi got to his feet and spat.

"I never needed a smoke so bad in my life," he said.

"Grass is matted down here," Jimbo said. He stalked forward, eyes fixed on the grass. "They moved downhill into the trees. Three paths joining into one."

Dwayne keyed the transmitter again.

"We're following a trail that leads west down toward a lake. Will report progress. Roenbach out."

"Should we risk calling out for them?" Chaz said.

"Not just yet. Jimbo, you're point."

Jimbo led the way, and the other three followed behind at twenty-foot intervals. They fell into the old routines of long-range patrol that had gotten them into and out of so many bad places intact so many times before. Jimbo studied the ground ahead and the others watched all about, weapons ready. There was cawing of birds coming from the trees below punctuated by louder squawks. Not sounds any of them recognized.

They moved into the shade of the tree line. There were clumps of broad-leafed ferns carpeting the forest floor. And the trunks of the trees were thick with fungi. There were enough broken or trampled-down ferns to provide a trail. When that failed, there were places where the fungi were crumbled, like someone rested against a tree bole or touched a hand to the tree at shoulder-height. Jimbo was able to lead them swiftly down the slope on a pathway that curved steadily down and joined a gully formed by runoff from past rainstorms. It was dry as dust now, no recent rains. A good thing for the Rangers. Any sign they could find from Caroline Tauber and company would be useful, and dry ground was the perfect medium for tracking.

Long pine needles rained on Dwayne from above. He looked up to see small animals drifting from tree to tree above. They made no sound, not even the thrum of wings.

"Bats?" Chaz narrowed his eyes and peered up.

"Squirrels," Dwayne said.

They were red squirrels with long thin tails and white bellies. They glided from tree to tree on wing membranes stretched between their fore and hind legs. Without a sound, they soared across the open areas of sky between trees. They vanished into the thick boughs of pine.

"Has to be hundreds of 'em," Renzi said. "Big fuckers," Chaz said.

As quickly as they appeared, all the squirrels were gone. A snapping of foliage and a low grunting noise came through the trees from below. Something big was moving around in the deep, deep woods.

Fingers slid from trigger guards. Safeties snapped off. Guns up and trained toward the sounds from below. The unseen source of the noise snuffled somewhere close. It made a final bleating noise and then could be heard moving away. The sounds of its passage fading as it moved away down the slope to their left.

The men stayed still until the cawing of the unseen birds returned.

"Any idea what that was?" Chaz said. He lowered his weapon.

"The doc said that most of the animals here will be bigger versions of ones we know," Dwayne said.

"My boy has picture books of prehistoric mammals," Renzi said. "Wolves the size of bears. Bears the size of elephants."

"Yeah, and real elephants," Dwayne said. "Doc said there could be elephants."

"What size are they in your boy's book, Ricky?" Chaz said.

"I dunno. Fucking huge." Renzi shrugged. Jimbo dropped to hands and knees again.

He ran fingers over the bed of brown needles that carpeted the ground. The ferns were thinning out.

"They came this way," Jimbo said. "How long ago?" Dwayne said.

"Six hours or more," Jimbo said. "But the trail's gonna be hard to follow over these needles."

Renzi spat again.

"Six hours or more?" Renzi said. "Even amateurs could be ten miles or more away from here by now. They could be anywhere."

"I'd say, given the odds, the doc got us pretty damned close," Chaz said.

"Look, the text said they had to hide," Dwayne said. "We make our way downhill and look for likely hiding spots. They didn't have time enough between their arrival and the text transmission to get very far from here."

They found a likely hiding spot twenty minutes down the slope, a collection of rocks and deadfall forming a natural half-circle which would offer some concealment. They found the broken wreckage of a wave transmitter much like the one Dwayne carried. It lay next to a headless human torso wearing a Batman t-shirt.

"No animal did this," Jimbo said. He squatted by the corpse. "Predators eat from the ass-end in. They don't bite parts off and take 'em away. Not a lot of blood around. They took the head first and did the rest when he was dead."

Dwayne crouched by him. Chaz and Renzi took positions just

up the hill and scanned the trees all around for movement and sound.

Bugs had been at the torso. Giant, horned beetles. Ants the length of a thumb. Flies were gathered in a cloud over a sticky pool of black blood that collected where the head should be. There was blood spray on the rocks. The neck ended in a raw wound with the white ends of vertebrae showing in a mess. The arms were gone at the shoulder. The legs at the hips. "Something chopped off his extremities,"

Jimbo said. "A blade of some kind. Not very sharp. But sharp enough."

"Not just one really huge critter taking big bites?" Dwayne said.

"No animal is this systematic," Jimbo said, shaking his head. "Anything that big would have dragged him away whole. Anything smaller would have torn his guts free. The torso's still intact. And you can see where a blade hit the thigh bone that's left here. There are angular chips out of it that a blade would make. Teeth make scrapes and splinters. It took about six chops to get through there."

"So the doc's research is off." Dwayne stood up.

"Yeah," Jimbo said. "There's people in these woods."

"Why'd they leave part of him?"

"Damned if I know." Jimbo shrugged.

"What was his name?" Chaz said.

"Phillip something," Dwayne said.

From the remains of Phillip Something, Jimbo could easily follow the trail. It looked to him like a dozen or more people with bare feet. There were long gouges in the ground that meant they were dragging two more figures. The captives were ambulatory but unwilling traveling companions. Caroline and Kemp.

"They alive, or did whoever took him drag away dead weight?" Chaz said. They were humping downhill in a tight diamond shape formation, six paces apart from each other. Defensive positions.

"Could be alive," Jimbo said. "Looks like whoever's dragging them is having a hard time of it here and there. You can see gouges in the dirt where needles have been kicked away. They're not going easy."

Jimbo crouched and studied the ground. "What else?" Dwayne said.

"Circular holes an inch or more across poked in the dirt either side of the trail. The captors were carrying spears or some other kind of poles. They used them to support their weight."

"Sun's goin' down, Dwayne," Renzi said. He was walking drag —watching their six o'clock. "We just gonna run right up on 'em?"

Dwayne held a hand up and hissed. All stopped. Guns up and eyes moving.

"Smell that?" he said.

"A wood fire," Chad said. "Real faint. Far off."

"A cook fire," Renzi said.

They broke into a trot through the trees.

A half-mile along, the terrain leveled out a bit as the slope of the hill decreased to twenty degrees. The smell of wood smoke was stronger now, and they abandoned any kind of tracking and moved directly toward the source. It was getting dark in a hurry. The sun was sinking. Pools of deep shadow formed between the trees. They crossed a broad, well-used trail that ran across the slope laterally and wound down toward the water. The surface was trodden flat by many feet over a long time.

The new trail brought them down the slope and out on a narrow strip of sand and rock where the sea lapped up in lazy rollers. A gentle susurration of surf and barely any chop to the water. The air was cooler coming off it. Renzi walked in ankle deep and stooped to cup his hand in the water.

"Salty," Renzi said. He spat out the taste of it. "Not as much as sea water. But there's salt."

"That's good," Dwayne said. "That means we probably won't run into anything coming down to take a drink."

"Ain't concerned with what comes *down* to the water," Chaz said. "But what might come *out* of it is a different story. We should have brought the Renzi kid's picture book with us."

Renzi jogged out of the water and back to the sand.

The narrow beach ran along a rock face and curved to the west around to a flinty point that jutted out into the water. The jagged point of land was backlit by a yellow glow in the deepening gloom. Behind those rocks was a massive fire of some kind. It threw light far out onto the water creating golden highlights atop the wavelets.

"Here's where they came out," Jimbo said. A double row of drag marks and lots of footprints led along the tree line toward the light of the fire. It was plain enough sign for any of them to recognize.

"Single file," Dwayne said. "Chaz, you're walkin' drag. Jimbo, on point."

It was full-on dark when they reached the rocky outcropping. A glow rose from the other side of the collection of craggy, volcanic boulders. The campfire. A big one or more than one. Thick white smoke was carried by the wind off the water and into the boughs of the pines on the ridgeline above them.

To get around the rocky formation, they waded into the warm water. One hand to the wall to steady them and one hand training their weapons forward as they moved. Dwayne took the lead. The first turn brought them onto a new strip of beach nestled in a cleft in the formation. What looked like single ridge was a series of natural jetties of volcanic rock running out into the water. They all had experience in this kind of country. The ridges were what was left by flows of lava from an eruption sometime in the past.

They spread like fingers into the water. As Dwayne rounded the first jetty of black rock and stepped out of the water. He found himself ten feet from a man squatting in the sand to take a dump.

For an instant, they stared at one another. The man was five feet in height, with broad shoulders and a thick neck almost as broad across as his head, thin legs and callous-covered feet. His upper body was corded muscle, and he was covered with filth that hid the true color of his skin. His dark matted hair hung in his face and down to his shoulders. There were shells and yellow stones braided into his hair in strands, and he wore a necklace with similar decorations. His features were broad and flat, and his mouth opened in surprise to reveal blackened teeth filed to points. He wore no clothing except a hide belt about his narrow hips from which hung an "L" shaped bit of carved bone secured by a loop of twine. There was a spear with a six-foot haft stuck point first in the sand by him.

The man locked eyes with Dwayne—huge yellowish eyes. He dropped a sudden stream of greasy shit between his feet and grabbed for his spear with an animal growl.

Dwayne rushed three strides and drove the butt of his rifle between the man's eyes. The blow lifted the lighter man off his bare feet. He fell to a motionless heap without a cry and into his own pile of stinking feces.

The others closed around to look at the thing lying in the sand. Dwayne's blow had crushed the skull in the front. The black, broad set eyes stared up at nothing. Dwayne trained his weapon up the beach, but there was no movement. There was a second ridge of rock separating this section of sand from the next part of the beach. The source of the glow was still out of sight behind the natural jetty.

"Is he an Indian or what?" Renzi said.

"No Indian ever looked like that," Jimbo said. "His nose is too flat. And the ears are small and low on the skull. And the eyes.

Those are bigger than any human I've ever seen. They're like animal eyes."

"Maybe he's an ugly Indian," Renzi said. He wrinkled his nose and touched a boot toe to the leg of the corpse.

"Maybe he's not human," Chaz said. "At least, not as human as us. Look at those teeth."

The slack mouth of the dead man revealed rows of long teeth coming to a point at the end. They were broad and stained dark, and there were just too damned many of them. The jawline protruded to contain them. The nose was wide, with thin nostrils that were more like slits.

"Whoever they are, they're human enough to have set out a picket," Dwayne said. "If Stinky here didn't have the trots, it'd be me lying there with a spear in my belly."

Jimbo crouched farther up the beach. "Trail picks up here."

They moved at a trot toward the next ridge of rocks. A sandy trail led up to a saddle in the formation. Embers rose high into the air from the light source behind it. The smell of wood smoke stung their nostrils. They were close.

Dwayne signaled to the others with a hand flat and level to the ground. They dropped to their knees and crawled across the broad sand trail to take up positions in the porous rocks. The rocks would hide them. Anyone near that fire would have lost their night vision for sure. Chaz was by Dwayne as they crept through the dead brush between two upright spires of standing rock. Dwayne parted the dry brush and looked downhill.

The hillside was eroded away below them to make a near-vertical drop of a hundred feet or more. It formed a wide natural bowl with one side open to the water. It was more clearly defined than the defile they saw from their vantage point atop the mesa back in The Now.

A bonfire roared down in the bowl. They could feel the heat of it on their faces from two hundred feet away. A big blaze feeding on logs stacked ten feet high. Glowing embers and white smoke were carried by the wind off the lake. The beach backed up on a cliff face and, in the center of it was a broad cave opening that was wide at the bottom, thin at the top like an inverted "V," and forty feet across. An enormous skull hung over the entrance at the top of the cave. An elephant. Had to be. Long, curved tusks jutted from the mouth and reflected the blaze. Firelight came from within the cave. Smoke drifted up through the rock above. A natural chimney.

All around the broad, flat area, were crude huts of stacked timbers and mud wattle arranged in no particular pattern. It looked like hundreds of hooches, but the dark beyond the fire-light hid the full extent of the settlement. These hovels were roofed with bundles of reeds and decorated with bones and shells. Around the huts were untidy stacks of bones, shells, and kindling. Animal skins were stretched on crude tanning racks. Some of them were from pretty sizeable critters. There were curved tusks piled high. Some of the tusks looked like they were ten feet long, minimum.

In the light of the flames, figures moved. They were human, or like humans. The distance and the uncertain, flickering light hid any details. They walked upright, or mostly upright. They made a peculiar hopping motion that raised the hairs on the back of Dwayne's neck.

There were smaller ones, children, running around. Small dogs yapped at their heels. Some of the figures used sticks to stoke the fire.

Dwayne and Chaz backed out ass-first from their hide. Renzi and Jimbo joined them in the shelter of the rocks.

"A goat-fuck," Renzi said.

"And we're the goats," Chaz said.

"Quiet." Dwayne had the transmitter out and keyed it. "Roen-bach to Tauber. Mission time oh-one-twenty-two. We are at a half-ring formation of rock with a cave at its base. I'd say three klicks west/northwest from insertion point. The cave opening is on the north face of the escarpment. We found an encampment of humans. Roenbach out."

"There weren't supposed to be people," Jimbo said. "The doc said there was no fossil record of people in Nevada in this age. Now there's hundreds of them down there. Maybe more. A freakin' town full of 'em."

"Not any record anyone *found*," Dwayne said. "That means the bones of whoever's down there are probably lying out behind the compound waiting to be found. I read up on these Paleo-Indians. Anthropologists keep moving the arrival of humans in North America back all the time. They're off by forty thousand years, turns out."

"Told you they weren't Indians," Jimbo said. "Some kind of missing links or evolutionary dead end."

Renzi pulled the curved piece of bone he'd taken from the dead man's belt and inspected it. "It's a woomera," he said. "A tool for getting more loft out of a spear. I saw Aborigines use them in Australia."

"On cable?" Chaz said.

"In Australia," Renzi said. He held a middle finger up to Chaz.

"What's our next move?" Chaz said.

The sound of a high, shrill, shrieking voice coming from the fire below decided that for them. It was someone shouting. Loud and clear. In English.

"For God's sake! No!"

Dwayne clambered to the top of the rocks and looked down into the bowl.

A clutch of figures was moving at the opening of that cave. The voice, a female voice, was coming from that direction. Words lost on the wind but clearly English. Some of the figures moved away from the fire toward the cave. He pulled his pair of eco-friendly binoculars from his bag and trained them on the source of the voice.

Among the dark figures were two people who seemed to glow

in the firelight in contrast to the darker figures crowded around them. The 10x binocs were weak but allowed Dwayne to pick out a naked man and woman in the midst of a growing gang of the camp's inhabitants. They were taller than the skinnies massed around them. Humans. Real hundred-percent human beings.

The woman gleamed in the light. She was painted head to toe with some kind of lime wash that gave her a ghostly appearance. Her hair was stiff with lime, and there were necklaces strung with stones around her neck. Some of them glittered in the fire-light. Her eyes appeared like two motionless black holes. Dwayne feared she'd been blinded, but a closer look revealed that her eyes were painted all around with some kind of black substance.

It was Caroline Tauber, and she was shouting in anger, not fear, and backing away with her fists raised for a fight. The man, Dr. Miles Kemp, was in the grip of a half-dozen of the dark men. He was more than a head taller than the tallest of them but could not break away from them. They were placing some kind of lariat over his neck. Then another. Two of the squat figures yanked him toward the fire on leads. He fell, and they dragged him. He wrenched at the rope choking him and kicked the sand.

Caroline backed toward the cliff wall and aimed a kick at one of her captors. They seemed more amused than anything else. They danced around her, waving their arms and feinting leaps at her. One got too close. She drove the heel of her hand into his face, and the bastard fell hard. She stomped on him two or three times, and he folded up. The fun was over. Dozens of them rushed her at once and dragged her back into the cave, scream-ing. No weapons were raised, but no one struck her while an old, old woman shrieked and gestured at them.

Kemp was on his hands and knees, being pulled like a dog on a leash toward the fire. The mob waiting there hooted, made cat-calls and slapped palms on their thighs. They were happy about something, and that couldn't be good.

Dwayne ran sliding down the trail of soft sand and motioned for the other three to follow him.

They stayed as much to the shadows as the firelight would allow. Dwayne took lead and brought them from cover to cover at a trot. A steep pathway brought them down and around the edge of the depression where the dark was deepest.

The cries from below continued. They were recognizable as the voice of a man. It had to be Kemp. He was wailing and pleading hysterically. Jesus figured big in his pleading, but Jesus was a hundred thousand years away.

The other three closed up behind Dwayne. He gestured forward with closed fingers. They moved hunched over, duck-walking past the stacks of firewood, bone, ivory and the stinking skins stretched on wooden frames. Some of those stacks they passed were skulls. The skulls of creatures damned close to human. The four men had their rifles shouldered. From here on, their total focus was on whatever they saw over their gunsights. The world they could see was a kill zone.

Figures were clustered around Dr. Miles Kemp at the edge of the huge bonfire. The doctor's naked white flesh made him stand out in the crowd of dark men and women bunched around him. He was secured by braided leather thongs tied around his neck like a collar and leash. His arms were gripped tight by the yammering figures that clustered all around. There were dark bruises on his arms and legs, and one eye was swollen shut where he'd been struck. The mob stood cackling and clapping their hands on their thighs as Kemp begged them to let him go. Some of the males, painted in stripes of white and red, blew on hunting horns made from the hollowed points of tusks. The children threw handfuls of sand. Kemp mewled in a keening ramble interrupted by convulsive sobs. One of the captors slapped Kemp's belly to make the fat jiggle. This resulted in more hooting sounds from the crowd. Many of them held long spears tipped with stone blades like the one the shitter on the beach had. Others held clubs made of the long leg bone of some animal, with sharpened flint blades bound in a notch at one end with leather strips.

Kemp was brought to the ground by his captors. Adults and children sat on his arms and legs to hold him still. It was hard to tell male from female. All were emaciated, with stringy muscles over bony frames.

The close-packed mob parted to allow a figure to step closer to the struggling Kemp. This new arrival was painted head to toe in lime just as Caroline Tauber was. His body shone white in the light of the fire. He had a broad stripe of crimson painted over his eyes like a mask. He wore a tall headdress of feathers bound to his scalp with braids of hair dotted with those yellow stones. About his neck hung an amulet on a thong. It was crudely fashioned in the shape of a running animal of some species. The firelight caught it, and it gleamed as he moved.

The white-painted man crouched by the wriggling and pleading Kemp. The doctor flinched and stopped his begging, breathless, as the man touched the beard on his face. The painted man's touch was gentle at first. Then he began roughly pulling at Kemp's face. The feathered man tugged at the hairs as though to tear them from Kemp's face. Kemp howled and wept. He was making sounds now but not words. There weren't any more words for what he wanted to say.

Satisfied that the beard was permanently attached, the white-painted man released Kemp. He picked up a handful of cold ashes from near the fire and swiped them in a ragged line down Kemp's chest from sternum to crotch so that a black line of soot bisected Kemp's torso top to bottom. This brought a cooing sound from the crowd. They pressed closer and then backed away. It was a ritual they all knew well.

A new figure stepped into the firelight. This one was painted red over every bit of exposed flesh, some kind of clay smeared over every inch of him. He wore strands of necklaces made of what looked like finger bones around his throat. He was more thickly muscled than the others and wore his hair swept back and caked with tar or sap. His eyes were large black orbs and set wide. In his fist, he carried a stone ax with a broad head and sharply chiseled edge set in a thick wooden handle bound in leather strapping.

The ax man walked forward and planted a foot in the sand on either side of Kemp's hips. He spat a thick stream of saliva onto Kemp's belly then raised the ax over his head in both hands. The muscles of his shoulders bunched. His mouth spread in a grin filled with rows of pointed black teeth. His eyes opened wide with whites showing. The crowd around him took in a breath with a single loud gasp.

A short hissing sound was followed by another.

Then the red-painted man's head popped loudly, throwing his blood and brains in a spray over the anxious mob.

Jimbo and Renzi followed their first aimed shots with covering fire from atop a stack of firewood. They fired at the dude with the feather hat right after the axman, but the white-painted bastard leaped out of sight, and the shots went wide. They swept the mob around Kemp with rapid fire. Bodies fell or stumbled away. The rocket projectiles made wounds similar to a rifled slug from a 12-gauge. It lifted targets clean off their feet, blood and bone spraying everywhere. One bastard went sailing straight into the bonfire. He lay convulsing in the blaze and cooked. The explosive rounds were even more devastating and sent showers of hot shrapnel into the screaming mass.

Dwayne trotted toward the fire with Chaz on his heels. They picked off a few spearmen between them and Kemp. Dogs barked and showed teeth. Dwayne put a round through one that sent it spinning away in two pieces. The dogs backed down with a series of long high squeals. They vanished across the sand and into the dark.

Unlike the mutts, the blood-spattered mob was restless but not moving away. They bared teeth and swayed from foot to foot like animals before a charge.

"What's wrong with the skinnies?" Chaz said. "They should be scared shitless by now." Chaz reverted without a thought to the term "skinnies," the generic term for foreign hostiles who were invariably thinner and shorter than US troops.

"Well, they're not," Dwayne said. He let go with a triple burst at the spearmen massed around Kemp. The slow discharge followed by the rapid trajectory of the missiles took some getting used to.

Some of the skinnies still stood on Kemp's arms and legs to keep the doctor pressed to the ground. Even as fire from the four rifles brought them down, they were replaced by others screaming defiance and showing filed teeth. They weren't going to give away their prize that easy.

The spearmen pulled at the hooked bits of carved bone they all wore on their belts and fixed the butt end of their spears to carved notches at the crook of the devices.

With the spears resting in the bone crooks, the men began to throw them in an underhand lob with all their weight behind it. Dwayne and Chaz threw themselves to the sand as spears whistled by close above them. They each took turns firing long volleys from the prone position as the other reloaded. The clutch of spear throwers wouldn't give up their prisoner and stayed in a phalanx no matter how many fell. Kemp howled as bodies fell on him in a heap. Some men with clubs and spears were moving away from the fire to flank Dwayne and Chaz.

"The guns are too damn quiet!" Chaz said. He turned on his side and drilled a few of the circling men. The others ran out of sight behind the cover of a hut. "We need some noise! Some fucking noise!"

Dwayne rolled on his back and called out. "Renzi!"

A satchel charge sailed over the heads of the spearmen with none of them noticing. The clutch of enraged skinnies was solely focused on Dwayne and Chaz. The Semtex bundle exploded in the middle of the bonfire with a force that sent burning logs spinning end over end in all directions. The fire spread across the ground and ignited dozens in the shrieking crowd. Blazing logs crashed into huts and set them afire. This was finally enough to throw the spearmen off their game, but not before one drove the stone head of his spear deep into Kemp's gut. Kemp convulsed with an animal howl. A triple-tap from Dwayne sent the bastard with the spear flying away, ripped open like a piñata.

A second satchel charge landed on the other side of the fire and shook the ground when it went off. The crowd of hooting spearmen and their kin backed away into the dark making low moans of what Dwayne hoped was terror.

Jimbo joined them at a run as Dwayne and Chaz reached Kemp. The man was in bad shape. The broken end of the spear nailed him to the ground through the gut. He was wide-eyed and gasping. Blood sprayed from his mouth with each panicked breath.

They started to move him, and he screamed. "He's not going to make it," Chaz said.

"And we're down to our last magazines."

Dwayne dropped down next to Kemp. He put his face close to the other man's.

Kemp blinked. His eyes moved in his head. He moved his lips. Blood spilled in thick strands from his mouth and nostrils, then his eyes were no longer seeing anything.

"Dwayne," Chaz said

"We move for the cave," Dwayne said. "While they're still disoriented."

7

DR. MORRIS TAUBER

The flash of blue light was different than the sheet lightning that sometimes illuminated the valley floor in the hours just before dawn. The resounding boom of thunder echoed among the rocks atop the mesa and was a long time dying away.

Inside the refrigerated chamber, Tauber was watching, squinting into the thick white mist rolling from inside the Tube's frame as the field opened again. Nothing emerged. It was two days since the team of four Rangers had walked into the array of frozen coils.

Tauber stood for moments with his jaw clenched tight. It was an opening to a world he could only dream of, a world he populated with dark imaginings. The weeks of worry over the fate of Caroline were taking their toll.

"Idiot," he said. He moved quickly to the computer station, where he fine-tuned the power levels from the tower to the Tube. He moved the mouse to bring the feed into the parameters his calculations determined were the right ones for keeping the field open within the target time frame. Attuned correctly he could hold the door open for thirty minutes maximum.

He opened the program for the wave transmitter and turned

up the gain. The indicator showed that there was a recorded message coming through.

It was Dwayne's voice. It came from the speakers with a heavy background hiss.

"Roenbach to Tauber. Mission time oh-one-twenty-two. We are at...formation of rock with a cave at its base...three klicks west/northwest...from...point...found an encampment of humans...bach out."

The transmission was faint and spotty, but Tauber could run it through audio programs later to clean it up. The message would also repeat for as long as the field was open. He'd put it all together later. As long as the transmitter kept sending fresh messages, there was hope.

An hour and twenty minutes from their arrival? Had they found anything? He wondered what the mission time was now relative to this most recent field breach and was determined to work out some kind of program to correlate the time on the other end of the field as related to time in The Now with each field opening. Some kind of time check transmission that would update every sixty seconds.

Back in the past, it could be an hour after Dwayne recorded the message or it could be days. It was maddening. Not for the first time did Tauber consider running into the Tube and going into the past, just for a peek, just for some confirmation. He could run back to the present, and no harm done. But if the field was not as stable as he thought, if it collapsed while he was in prehistoric Nevada or while he was in transit...

No, he realized, he was useful to Caroline and the others on this side of the Tube. The men he hired were the best chance to bring his sister and her colleagues back alive. His job was here manning the controls and making sure Parviz and Quebat kept the reactor at maximum efficiency.

The ambient noise made by the Tube faded to silence. The cloud of frozen gas thinned away to a light mist. The field was closed and would not reopen for two days when the reactor was at optimal output again. Tauber was alone with his fears again for forty-eight hours.

The only thing for it was to stay busy. He had a full two days to worry and he wasn't going to start now. Work was the remedy, work, or fall into a blue, disabling depression. Caroline would never give up like that, Tauber told himself. He thought of making another call on the satellite phone but decided against it. No reason to let their benefactor know that the crisis continued. Tauber might need more favors if there were still any favors to be had.

Time and money. Money and time. One was limited in supply. The other was malleable and fluid but still beyond his ability to control with any real precision.

He ran the last audio transmission from Roenbach through the filters and listened to it a dozen times over until he'd pieced it together. He wrote it down on a legal pad word for word.

Roenbach to Tauber. Mission time oh-one-twenty-two. We are at a half-ring formation of rock with a cave at its base. I'd say three klicks west/northwest from insertion point. The cave opening is on the north face of the escarpment. We found an encampment of humans. Roenbach out.

Humans? Was that possible? Were the chronometric readings off and the Tube opened a field in the wrong era? If there was an indigenous aboriginal population in the time frame that Caroline and the others entered, it would explain a lot. If only Dwayne left a more detailed message.

Tauber thought again how his sister, Phillip, and Martin were no more than a forty-five-minute hike from where he stood, separated from safety by a gulf of millennia.

He left the buried Tube chamber and stepped blinking into the blast of desert sun. Parviz and Quebat were exiting the reactor hut in their rad suits. Parviz turned the spigot on a faucet and began spraying Quebat with a garden hose. It was a rough and ready way of cleaning as much of the stray radiation off them as possible. Parviz, the more adept at English, constantly assured Tauber that this was adequate.

"The rocks all around us give off as many rems as we are releasing," Parviz would say as though Tauber were a child. "There are no worries. Hosing off a precaution only."

Tauber stood by waiting as they hosed each other down and then stripped off the Tyvek coveralls and dropped them into a steel oil drum. They were in boxers and t-shirts. Quebat's shirt said What Happens In Vegas . . . Tauber didn't approach until Parviz had ignited the discarded suits with lighter fluid and set them ablaze.

He joined them as they walked to the community hut.

"Any good lucks, Dr. Tauber?" Parviz said.

He asked the same question each time.

"Only a transmission from Mr. Roenbach," Tauber said. "They made it through and gave me their current position. Well, relative to..." He trailed away. This whole enterprise lacked its own language. How to convey the complexities of dealing with two planes of time progressing at different rates in relation to one another?

"They okay, then? So far so good, then?" Parviz said. That about summed it up.

"Look, can I talk to you guys?" Tauber said. They stopped as one and regarded him. "It's about the reactor," he said.

"Over breakfast, please?" Parviz said and held the door to the hut for Quebat.

Tauber had re-heated coffee from the night before. Parviz set the table and Quebat prepared *haleem*, a nauseating mixture of lamb chunks and oatmeal. The two sat and adorned some kind of crusty flatbread with a thick smear of butter while their bowls cooled.

"You had a question, Doctor?" Parviz said.

He took a bite of the bread.

"It's about the re-charge time," Tauber said and took a chair across from them. "I know we've discussed this before. But are you absolutely certain there's no way to step up the process? Can we carve some time out of the forty-eight-hour regimen?"

"The timetable was worked out by Caroline and me," Parviz said. He took a sip of tea and continued. "Her requirements were sixty million volts at a sustained, controlled amperage of two hundred thousand amperes."

"Yes," Tauber said.

"Were you an engineer, I mean a *nuclear* engineer, you would understand better the balance we must achieve and how difficult it is to manage and maintain."

"Yes."

"The reactor is small, and it takes time to build to the levels necessary to activate the tower. Forty-eight hours is the very limit, the absolute minimum, as your sister calculated based on my findings. Pushing for higher levels in a shorter amount of time reduces the reactor's life and refueling it is problematic to say the very least, yes?"

"Yes."

"We understand what hardship this is. Very anxiety-making, Doctor."

Quebat wiped his mouth with a Hardee's napkin and said something in Persian.

"What was that?" Tauber said

"Quebat said that you must take comfort in knowing that whatever is to happen has already occurred long ago," Parviz said and reached for a jar of jam.

It took Tauber the rest of the day to find the location detailed in Roenbach's last transmission. He found it as the sun was setting. It was a half-circle of wind-smoothed volcanic rock with a cleft in the face at its center, the base of what was probably a volcanic remnant at one time, the edge of a rocky coastline. Now it was just a hump of granite and gypsum. The half-circle was dotted with clumps of Joshua, brittlebush, yucca, and sage. This was it. This place was where Caroline and the others found themselves a thousand centuries ago.

The sun was sinking fast. Tauber parked the Land Rover with its rack of lights aimed at the cave opening. On hands and knees, he crawled over a hump of sand at the cave's mouth and down a slope into the dark. A powerful handheld flash showed him the interior. The cave opened broader inside and was floored with fine silt blown in here over the millennia, some of it probably washed in here by storm surges on the great inland sea that once lay just outside the cave opening. The sea emptied sometime in the distant past during one tectonic upheaval or another.

The stark glare of his flashlight revealed no sign of any human habitation. That would be below him, under the silt. The floor of the cave as it was occupied by the people of the time could be twenty feet or more beneath his boot soles. He'd come back and dig. He wasn't sure why but he knew he'd come back and dig. It was something to do other than waiting, a way of connecting to the events unseen and unknowable on the other end of the Tube.

It wasn't until Tauber was halfway back to the compound, driving under the light of a half-moon, that he realized he'd just crawled on his belly into a dark desert cave that might have been inhabited by anything from a nest of angry rattlers to a coven of rabid bats or a pack of half-starved coyotes. He shivered at the wheel then smiled. It wasn't fear, it was anticipation. He'd come back tomorrow. He'd have all day, and rather than simply wait for the Iranians to crank up the reactor he'd have something to *do*.

The following day Tauber winched the backhoe onto its trailer and hitched it behind the Land Rover. The service road off the mesa ended at a dry wash, and this generally led west and north, so he followed that within a quarter-mile of the cave opening. From there he drove up the bank and slowly picked his way between rocks and around thick tangles of brush. It would be a long, hot walk back if he got stuck out here.

He reached the cave and quickly had the backhoe off the trailer. He wasn't terribly adept at operating it. Caroline and Phil had done most of the digging to cover the building that housed the Tube. But he soon had a handle on how the levers and pedals worked and spent the hottest part of the day pulling sand and rock away from the cave opening to make an easier passage.

He created an entrance large enough to let the hoe's arm inside the cave and carefully as he could Tauber scraped back at the fine silt within to reach the lower tiers of gravelly soil. Tauber got off the hoe and crouched to examine what he was digging up. Beneath the top layer of silt were strata of grainier stuff. He ran some though his fingers. Crushed shell and rounded stones that the sea had washed in here at some point in some long-ago storm surge.

The cave was filling with shadows as the sun dropped behind the hump of rock above. He should have brought work lights. He could keep going under the glare of the headlamps on the backhoe, but that was asking for trouble. If he had an accident, Parviz and Quebat would have no idea where he was or even that he was missing until he'd died of thirst and been eaten by the local wildlife.

He left the backhoe where it was and drove back in the dark to the compound. He could see the glow of the pole lamps atop the mesa from the wash and followed the light back to the service road. If there were no positive results when he re-opened the field in the morning, he'd come back and dig further. In its own way, it was a method of reaching out to Caroline that seemed more real to him right now than the promise of the Tube.

The following day brought nothing from the Tube. Not a

sound. Not a text. Not a hint of what was going on at the other end of the field.

Another sullen breakfast with the Iranians. Tauber pushed some eggs around a plate until they were rubbery and cold.

"Maybe you would enjoy going to Las Vegas along with us," Parviz said. "See a show and get your mind from your troubles."

"Michael Buble," Quebat said.

"I have something I have to do," Tauber said.

"In desert?" Parviz said. "What is there to do for two days in desert? You were gone until after dark."

Tauber explained about the message from Roenbach, the half-circle rock face, and the cave. *Soto voce*, Parviz translated the parts for Quebat that the other man could not follow with his unsteady grasp of English.

"We will help," Parviz said. Quebat nodded.

"Are you sure?" Tauber said.

"Buble is there all month," Parviz said.

At the cave site, Parviz operated the digital wire locator they used when they were running cable from the reactor hut to the tower and back. It was a long electronic wand that used sound waves and a magnetic resonance field to show them what was beneath the ground—a high tech divining rod. It was three feet long with a broad plastic body. An arm at the top supported a digital monitor for visuals of what had been detected. There was also audio, a wide range of beeps, buzzes, and hums that alerted the user to the proximity of buried objects and their depth beneath the soil.

The screen read nothing but a jumble of rocks beneath the scree of sand and shell, but it had an outside range of six feet. The three of them worked in the broiling sun using the backhoe. When the going got tight, they used shovels to remove more of the silt and gravel to allow the backhoe arm further access. None of them were archeologists. They were playing this by ear. The Iranians seemed to enjoy themselves. They even smiled a few times. Tauber assumed it was a relief to have a change from being cloistered with a reactor all day watching the clock. Even manual labor in the desert heat was a break for them.

The sun was setting, so they set up bright work lights inside and out of the cave opening and kept scraping away at the silt until they had deepened the floor of the cave by ten feet. Quebat had made sandwiches for them. Lamb for the Iranians and tuna salad with lettuce for Tauber. There were cold beers on ice in a cooler and hard lemonade, a favorite of Quebat's.

Parviz got a ping on the locator and waved it over an area of the floor against the back wall of the cave. The digital image showed a blurry, speckled picture of what looked like human skeletal remains at a depth of four feet.

On hands and knees, they scraped carefully at the layer of cool sand they'd uncovered. They used their fingers and the blades of trowels. It was past midnight, and there was a chill in the air by the time they found the first bones, a collection of ribs. They dug more gingerly now. It was Quebat who thought of using the melted ice from the cooler to wash the sand away from the bones. He poured the water on the cleared area and the hard packed grit began to melt away to reveal bones dried yellow and brown. There was evidence of three skeletons lying close together. They were surprisingly intact. The joints had long ago decayed and the structure collapsed but they were still in the rough arrangement that approximated how they must have looked in life. No animals had gotten to them. Perhaps they'd been buried in the silt of that long-ago storm surge.

Tauber recalled watching a special on TV about Pompeii and how the eruption of Vesuvius froze the dead in the postures in which they'd died. Perhaps the same had happened here in a sudden wash of silt and shell rather than volcanic ash.

Parviz trained the lights on the remains and Tauber brushed sand from the brittle bones with his fingers. The sand was still discolored here from the flesh and sinew that had sloughed off the trio all those years past. It was a rusty brown color.

The skulls of two of the remains were broad. The teeth that remained in the jaws were unusual. They were pointed as though they'd been filed and burnished purple-black. The skeletons appeared to belong to adolescents except for the exceptionally wide scapula. Well under five feet tall. And the long bones showed signs of bumps and lesions. Tauber knew from his casual reading of archeological magazines that these were indications of a short, brutal life, typical of remains found from Neolithic cultures.

Tauber lay on his belly in the glare of the lamps and spread sand away from the third skull of the skeleton that lay under the other two. This one was taller, the bones finer and unmarked. He whisked the sand from the visage of the skull. Its jaw was unhinged. These teeth were not filed. They were straight and unmarred and stained over time to a uniform color of dried corn.

All but one tooth that was still a translucent white. The second molar that Caroline lost in college when a pizza crust at a sorority party turned out to have a small pebble in it.

Tauber was gasping to breathe, and his vision blurred with tears as he brushed the last of the sand away from the skull to find a single round hole drilled in the left temple.

The next day, two of the men he'd sent down the Tube returned from the past.

8

MISSION CREEP

The village was ablaze. The satchel charge tossed into the bonfire threw flames over the huts and the rooftops of dry reeds turned the huts to pyres within seconds. The skinnies ran through the crazed shadow shooting and shrieking. Smoke hung thick in the air. It stung the eyes, and made it hard to breathe.

Dwayne led the Rangers through an outer ring of huts toward the wide cave opening. The huts were arranged with no discernible pattern, a random arrangement that didn't allow for easy navigation.

Spears and rocks came at them from all sides. Skinnies leaped from cover to taunt them with animal barks. The males used every opening to fling spears. The worst were the children who flung rocks, shells, and feces in a constant rain on the Rangers. And there were hundreds of the little bastards laughing and throwing their projectiles with astonishing accuracy.

Renzi fell to his knees when a rock struck him in the back of the head. Chaz dropped to a knee by him and poured a long burst of rocket rounds into the dark. The villagers leaped to cover behind their hooches. Rocket rounds ripped through the mud and wattle to dismember and disembowel. Chaz swung the barrel and sent a volley through a row of huts. He smiled when he heard screams from behind the structures.

"Shoot through the hooches!" Chaz said. "Through the walls!"

Dwayne and Jimbo fired rockets through the walls of the nearest structures. The hoots and catcalls turned to wails of fear and howls of agony. The storm of projectiles died away.

Chaz pulled Renzi to his feet. "You okay, bro?" Chaz said.

"I can hack it!" Renzi said. He pulled his arm from Chaz's grip. He yanked a satchel charge from his shoulder and pulled the fuse ring.

"Fire in the hole!" Renzi flung the satchel underhand into one of the larger huts in their path. All four men dove for the sand and covered their ears. They held their mouths open wide to lessen the pressure effects on their skulls.

The flimsy structure instantly turned into a storm of flying splinters and bone shards. Villagers using the hut for cover were shredded to strings of meat. Others fell concussed all around The rest scattered as if a hurricane wind had blown them away.

"This is insane!" Renzi shouted as he rose. He had a hand to the back of his head. Blood gleamed black in the firelight on his fingers. A thin stream ran from his left ear and down his neck.

"Caroline Tauber's in that cave," Dwayne said. "We can make it there while they're still shook up by the blast."

"Man, these skinnies don't scare so easy," Jimbo said. "They'll be back and more pissed off than before."

"All the more reason to hurry our asses then," Chaz said. He trotted after Dwayne, who was making his way toward the cave mouth visible beyond another row of huts. Villagers were already gathering again. Knots of them could be seen closing together in rough ranks in the flickering light. Chaz looked behind them and saw nothing but the burning huts and all around them the bodies of adults and children caught in the explosion or knocked down by rocket rounds. Some were alive but not for long. They shrieked and clawed at the scorched sand.

On their flanks, skinnies ran from cover to cover. They were moving alongside the four armed men, keeping pace. Everyone, villager and invader, was moving toward the cave mouth. They heard the bleat of horns resounding off the rocks above them. The skinnies were calling the whole neighborhood in on this. There was no way for the Rangers to know how large a force they could potentially be facing.

The four Rangers moved forward with fresh magazines. Each held his weapon firm to his shoulder and swept the area ahead. Villagers were gathering in a dense mob on the gradual slope of sand leading to the slit in the rock wall of the cliff. They stood swaying and muttering softly. Less than fifty yards to go to the cave opening.

Dwayne and Chaz picked off the closest spear carriers who dared to rush out from the crowd. Single shots on semi-auto. They were low on ammo and would need every round to get back to the mesa top and the field area of the Tube.

"Every one of these bastards and his cousin is here," Renzi said.

"No way through that," Jimbo said. "We're low on rounds and charges."

"We make a way," Dwayne said. "Everyone gives up when they've suffered enough. Even these sons of bitches."

"Renzi! Jimbo! Toss charges into them!" Dwayne planted his feet and sent a long burst into the massed villagers.

Renzi and Jimbo pulled the rings on the fuses and swung the satchels by the handles for the long toss. As if by a signal, a steady rain of rocks began pelting them from above. Above the cave mouth there were dozens of figures on ledges and outcrops, and all of them were lobbing stones at the four armed men. The figures called and jabbered and pried chunks of rock free to fling below. Their elongated shadows climbed the wall of the cliff face projected in stark contrast by the spreading flames of the burning village. The mass of hostiles before the cave mouth raised up a scream of defiance and started forward at a run.

No words were needed. It was time to withdraw. The four men began backing away toward the burning huts. Renzi and Jimbo threw their last charges as they backpedaled. They could feel the super-heated wind at their backs as they turned to run for the cover of the smoke drifting from the inferno.

The two satchel charges went off within seconds of each other, throwing skinnies in steaming bits into the air. Others were hammered to the ground. The twin blasts sent a concussive wave up the face of the rocks and dislodged a few rock throwers who fell screaming from their perches.

Back in the maze of huts, they began a more orderly withdrawal, two men covering the rear as two more re-loaded their weapons. Nothing slowed the pursuit of the skinnies. More spears were making it through the suppression fire. Villagers were running along either flank as well, flitting between huts soundlessly. The Rangers would be cut off from retreat if they couldn't get clear.

"Move it!" Dwayne shouted. "Bug the fuck out!"

All four men broke into an open run. They stayed in sight of one another, and all followed Dwayne, who fired wildly to either side of him while sprinting ahead. The crazy-quilt pattern of huts made them change direction several times, and only the growing howls of the mob closing in behind them kept them oriented. The village was larger than it looked when they first arrived. The dark beyond the bonfire hid the true expanse of it. It was a damned skinny metropolis.

They broke from the last ring of huts to find themselves on a long expanse of dark sand leading to the water. Villagers were rushing out onto the beach from huts to the left and right. It was darker here, farther from the flames. The numbers of skinnies were growing to either side and rushing toward them without a sound. The mob behind grew hushed as well. This was the kill, the endgame of the hunt. To the skinnies, the outcome was certain. They would run the Rangers to ground and finish them with spears and clubs and stones.

"We're ringed in," Chaz said. They were all out of breath from the run and coughing from the smoke in their lungs, their throats raw from it.

"Back toward the water," Dwayne said. He turned and began stepping toward the sound of gentle surf. The villagers emerged in a mass from the cover of the huts and onto the sand. Even the dogs had found their courage again and were yapping at their masters' feet. The mob formed a broad half-circle around the four men and started closing it up in a classic pincer movement. They were deliberate now. Their quarry was trapped. No need for haste or hysterics. Soon they'd have the intruders on a spit over their fire. The only advantage the Rangers had was the range of their weapons. But that edge would vanish if the skinnies rushed all at once.

"We make a last stand there?" Jimbo said. "At least I got to go to the beach," Renzi said. He spat on the sand.

"Look around you," Dwayne said. "You see any boats? Canoes? Dug-outs?"

Except for the scattering of bones and shells that marked the tide line the beach was empty all around.

"That means the little fuckers can't swim," Dwayne said. He unlimbered the last satchel charge he'd been carrying.

Spears began to fall around them. One landed with a thud by Jimbo's boot, its point buried deep in the sand. The range was closing.

"Run for the water," Dwayne said. He pulled the fuse ring of his last satchel and threw the charge in a high looping trajectory toward the growing mob of silhouetted shapes stalking closer.

The four men sprinted over the expanse of sand and reached the water just as the last satchel charge boomed behind them. They waded into the soft breakers with knees pumping. Chaz and Dwayne turned and fired suppression into the villagers just now reaching the water's edge. The Rangers were up to their waists with spears and rocks splashing into the water all around them. Each man lay back in the warm brine to reduce his target area. The villagers came no deeper than their knees into the swirling water. The skinnies went mad with frustration at the four men. They could see their quarry, but not reach them.

There was a surprisingly strong undertow, and the Rangers let it carry them from the shoreline and away into the darkness, stripping off gear and clothing as they went. Soon the enraged howling of the villagers and the yipping of their dogs faded away into the distance until all the four could hear was the lapping of the mild chop around them.

The current eventually carried them into shallow water they could stand up in, the level at their chests. Dawn light was beginning to show the outline of ridges to the north. Dwayne led the way, and the rest waded after him. The water had a slightly salty tang to it. There were rolling swirls on the surface near them and once or twice they were bumped by something unseen beneath the chop. Chaz wondered aloud what kind of fish might be in this water, but no one answered him.

They were down to the clothes on their backs. They'd stripped off ammo belts and other gear that might drag them down. Their rocket rifles were empty, and were discarded. All had dropped away to the bottom of the sea.

The sun was over the mesa as they splashed through still water that only came to their knees. They'd waded for miles as the lake floor rose at a slight grade, turning from sand and shale to gooey, clinging mud. The shoreline was marshy here and thick with reeds. They cut their arms to bleeding as they crashed through the saw-toothed fronds growing from the seabed. The mud sucked their boots off. They retrieved them from the muck and hung them around their necks by the laces.

Dragonflies with a wingspan as wide as a hubcap hovered just over the water. Flocks of birds that looked and sounded like geese exploded from the clumps of reeds as they neared.

Renzi fell hard with a splash and lay on his side.

"Move your ass, Ricky," Chaz growled. "Give me a minute," Renzi said and touched a hand to the patch of dried blood caked in his hair.

"You okay, bro?" Chaz crouched, his tone was softer.

"Dizzy," Renzi said. "Puked back there. It's a concussion."

"You lean on me, all right?" Chaz extended his hand.

"Stick that up your ass," Renzi said and rose to his knees. "I can hack it. I never needed help before."

"Then fuck it." Chaz jerked his hand back and stood up.

Dwayne slipped back between reeds and looked at them hard. He pulled Renzi to his feet. Renzi began to growl his thanks, and Dwayne put a hand to his mouth.

"Listen," Dwayne said.

The three men grew quiet. Jimbo stood point in the reeds ahead with his head up and listening hard. All around them they could hear the brittle crack of reeds being broken down. There was a soft sucking noise of movement in the mud. A snuffling sound, a gruff rattling exhalation of breath, came out of the reeds. A lot of somethings were making their way through the canes toward the open water. They were close enough to smell now. A rank, gamey smell.

A shadow fell over them as a shape loomed large over the reed tops.

"Don't. Run," Jimbo hissed and held a hand out to still them.

An elephant. A huge, hairy elephant. It stood in the muck looking down at them with one rolling eye. Two yellowing tusks swept the reeds over their heads as it swayed and the four men ducked low. The beast's trunk snaked toward them, making deep snorting sounds. The men stared at the enormous animal, transfixed. They could sense more large shapes moving slowly behind them, splashing through mud and trampling reeds in easy, deliberate progress.

The big bull mastodon made a sudden basso huffing sound and turned away from the Rangers. It moved away through the reeds and on toward the open water of the lake. The rest of the herd followed along, flattening reeds and churning the water a muddy brown.

Jimbo held a hand flat and lowered it toward the water.

"Slow," he said softly. The Rangers followed his example and moved away to the left to get out of the way of the lumbering animals.

They came out of the reeds and climbed a muddy slope to where a dense pine forest ringed the shoreline as far around as they could see. The slope was trampled to stinking muck with the passage of the elephant herd now standing somewhere out on the water. Their bleats echoed from somewhere out behind them. A misting rain had begun that reduced visibility to fifty yards in any direction.

Exhausted and chilled, they dropped to the forest floor.

"What now?" Chaz said with an arm thrown over his eyes.

"Inventory," Dwayne said and sat with his back against a tree bole.

It was a sad collection of gear that remained. No rifles or ammo. They had their *botas* and a few protein bars. The special wristwatches Doc Tauber was so proud of had gotten soaked, and the bands parted. The boots were nearly useless. The water had weakened the vegetable-based glue that held them together, and the soles and uppers were peeling apart. The socks were holding up surprisingly well, as were the BDUs.

"Find the two pairs of boots in the best shape," Dwayne said. "And save all the laces." The boot laces were leather and had lots of uses. They made a pathetic pile of soggy belongings.

"Now your holdouts," Dwayne said and met each man with a hard expression.

"What?" Chaz said. All innocence.

"Don't bullshit me," Dwayne said. "I've been with you guys too long. There's no way all of you followed the rules. Or *any* of you."

Jimbo shrugged and dug a six-inch clasp knife out of a cargo pocket on his leg. Renzi sat hunched forward with his head in his hands. "Yeah?"

"Give it up," Dwayne said, standing over him with his hand out.

"What the fuck you talkin' about?" Renzi's voice was a weak rasp, but the defiance was still there.

"You have a hideaway. You always have a hideaway."

Renzi reached into a cargo pocket, and his hand came back with a silver Zippo lighter engraved with RLTW (Rangers Lead The Way)

"Chaz?" Dwayne said.

Chaz dropped a black two-barrel derringer with rubber grips onto the pile.

Dwayne opened the derringer. Two .22 magnum rounds sat in place.

"Any more ammo, Chaz?" Dwayne said. "Naw." Chaz grinned. "Two rounds was enough to give me the last word."

They made a fire of pine needles and driftwood and banked it with earth all around to hide the glow. The smoke would be invisible in the misting drizzle that continued to fall. They stripped out of the BDUs down to skivvies and set the clothes around the fire to dry. Chaz washed Renzi's wound. There was a gash to his scalp, but the bleeding had slowed. His skull was intact but all the signs of head trauma were there. All Chaz could do was squirt some antibiotic gel on it and seal the cut with liquid bandage from the med kit. Renzi was fighting hard not to fall asleep or pass out. They were all wasted and appreciated how much harder their buddy was having it. They took turns prodding him awake.

None of them expected any kind of pursuit right away. The skinnies across the lake would still be licking their wounds after the hurt the Rangers put on them the night before. Depending on how motivated they were, the skinnies would eventually make their way around the shoreline looking for signs of where the four strangers emerged from the water. Or maybe the prehistoric assholes would just assume the four men had drowned as *they* would have if they entered water over their heads.

Dwayne cleared a patch of ground of pine needles and drew a rough circle in the dirt with a stick.

"We're somewhere on the north shore," he said and scratched an "x" in the dirt at the top of the circle. "The mesa and the compound are above the east shore. Somewhere...here." He waved the stick to the right of the drawing.

"Where the compound *will* be," Chaz added. "A long, long time from now."

"Like my head don't hurt enough already, you have to bring up that kind of shit," Renzi groaned.

"What's next?" Jimbo said and met Dwayne's eyes.

"You guys still want to follow my lead?" Dwayne regarded them. "I brought you into this clusterfuck."

"Don't be an asshole," Chaz said after a moment. The other two said nothing.

"Okay," Dwayne said. "Chaz, you're going to take Ricky out of here. And no shit from you, Ricky. You have a bruised brain and need it looked at. Chaz will bring you up to the mesa, and both of you wait for the field to open and go back to The Now. Jimbo and I will stay behind."

"To accomplish what, exactly?" Chaz said. "To stay on post," Jimbo said.

"Right. We can't just walk away now," Dwayne said. "They're holding the doc's sister. Me and Jimbo will set up a hide over the skinnies' camp and keep an eye on them."

"She's slow-roasting by now, Dwayne," Chaz said.

"I don't think so. They had her painted and strung her with necklaces. They didn't do that to their other kills, and they made sure they didn't kill her when she was trying to stop them from taking Kemp. They got her penned up in that cave for a purpose. They're worshipping her or something."

"Or she's part of a harem," Renzi said. "She's somebody's bitch by now."

"And if that's keeping her alive, then that's a good thing," Jimbo said.

"Easy for you to say," Renzi answered with a bitter laugh. "You're not playing house with one of those ugly motherfuckers."

"That's all between her and her therapist," Dwayne said. "Our problem is to get her home no matter what condition she's in. Me and Jimbo will keep post on the situation until you guys get back."

"And if things jump off before the cavalry gets here?" Chaz said.

"We'll deal with that when it gets here," Dwayne said. Chaz started to respond, but Dwayne held a hand up. "Yeah, as a plan it sucks cock. But this whole job's sucked from Day One, and I blame myself. We went in on someone else's mission parameters and rules of engagement. We agreed to shit gear and shit intel, and it's my fault we're in the spot we're in. Now the game changes, and it's our call on ordnance, rules, and how the job gets done."

"What do you need from me?" Chaz asked.

"You'll have forty-eight hours after you get back. You get the Iranians to drive Ricky to the nearest hospital. They can say he fell while hiking. It covers all his injuries. Then you trade favors, reach out to friends, and work your contacts to get us some serious firepower and get your ass back to us as soon as you can."

"So, we're going to war," Chaz said.

"Yeah."

"We'll need Hammond," Chaz said.

Dwayne drew triangles in the dirt.

"He has the contacts and the juice," Chaz said. "He can smooth the bumps. And he's good in corners like this. You *know* that, Dwayne."

Dwayne drew a couple more triangles in the dirt. He tossed the stick aside and stood.

"Call him when you get there," Dwayne said.

9

CAROLINE TAUBER

The guttering fire threw dancing shadows up the walls of the cave interior. An old, old, toothless woman crouched dozing in the glow, a stick decorated with feathers and small bones held loose in her hand. Furs and skins lay in messy piles about the fire where, most nights, the usual inhabitants of the cave slept and coupled in varying combinations. But the old crone had chased them all away to stand watch over Caroline by herself.

Caroline sat against the back wall of the cave with wrists bound tight behind her back with strips of leather. Her ankles were secured to a heavy length of log in the same way. She tugged at her bonds, but they only cut her skin. Her wrists and ankles were already torn and raw from the rough sinew thongs. She was weak from hunger and anxiety. Her body was one throbbing ache from the rough treatment at the hands of her captors, but she had no crippling injuries other than fatigue and, she strongly suspected, shock.

She rested her head back against the wall and twisted to one side to take the weight off her wrists and make herself as comfortable as was possible. She could see nothing past the fire and Old Mother fitfully napping there in the smoky gloom. But she could hear the sounds from outside. The tribe was wailing and screaming, and the unmistakable cries of the dying and wounded mixed with the grieving echoed into the cave.

The men who came for her from her own time punished the tribe harshly. The explosions that rocked the cave after they dragged her back inside told her that. She didn't know who the men were or how many. She could only surmise that her brother had sent them. She only caught a glimpse of men, men in some kind of military dress, moving in the uncertain light of the bonfire. Then the aborigines dragged her back in here and re-tied her wrists and bound down her ankles to the log. They left Old Mother behind to keep an eye on her. In fact, Old Mother hustled them out of the cave, spitting and waving her totem stick.

Caroline heard Miles Kemp's continuing cries for mercy, followed by the satisfied humming from the tribe. Then came the explosions and shouts, some of them in clear English. She heard the hunting horns being blown and shivered at the sound. The flickering light and stink of wood smoke told her that the village was burning, or much of it, anyway.

Old Mother looked frightened with wide eyes and spoke to Caroline in a wheedling, pleading tone. She clutched at Caroline, pawing at her lime-painted skin. The ancient hag knew the men were of the same type as her captive. Was she begging Caroline to call them off? Maybe she thought they were demons summoned by the newcomers for the purposes of bloody revenge. Caroline could make no sense of the mewling streaming from Old Moth-er's spittle-flecked lips. She only wished the stinking old crone would leave her alone.

The explosions and screams died down until the world beyond the cave mouth grew silent before the tribe's sorrow and rage found its voice. Caroline lay against the wall, her cheek pressed to the cool stone, and waited for whatever came next and thought about how she and Miles and Phillip came to be here.

A hunting party of men found them as they made their way down the slope away from the misty field of the Tube and toward the inland sea.

Was that really only this afternoon?

The first sign that they were not the only humanoids in the region were the horns. They heard the bleats sounding from the trees, bleats answered in kind from all around. Kemp was the first to suggest that they weren't animal noises but purposeful sounds made by artificial means. Caroline began to text about them when the strange, stout men stepped from the dark of the trees.

At first, the aborigines were an unexpected, but not unwelcome, surprise. The clutch of little dark men stood with spears held casually, not threatening. They seemed to be only mildly curious about the trio of strangers suddenly appearing on their hunting ground. Phillip Worth walked toward them with a smile and extended an open hand in friendship; a gesture that his anthropological studies told him was a universal sign of peaceful intentions.

The leader of the party, a man older than the rest and distinguished by a hood made of feathers and bone draped over his head, sniffed at the hand like a dog might and straightened to regard Phillip with narrowed eyes. He wore the hollow horn of some animal about his shoulder, suspended on a leather thong.

Caroline stood up the slope close by Miles and watched in silent fascination. These were proto-men; higher primates with as much physical resemblance to apes as they had to man. They used tools and wore rudimentary clothing. But their large eyes and pronounced teeth meant they were far from human. And if her calculations were on the mark and they were at 100,000 BC and change, these were not ancestors of modern man. Rather they were a failed evolutionary experiment that died out long before the first Paleo-Indians crossed over from Asia.

She realized that this was a paleozoological discovery of the century. Back in The Now she could lead a team to this valley and direct them to the strata they would need to uncover to find evidence of this lost race of hominids. Only she could never do that. The Tauber Tube was a technology the world could never know about.

Phillip thrust his hand out closer, and the leader took his wrist in a firm grip. Phillip smiled and pumped the leader's hand. The leader showed his teeth, black and filed to points, in what Phillip mistook as a smile. Phillip showed his own perfectly capped and whitened teeth in response. The little man's grip was surprisingly strong, and he increased the pressure on Phillip's wrist. He'd mistaken Phillip's shake and the baring of teeth for an attempt to escape and pulled hard to bring the young man stumbling toward him. Phillip fell to his knees.

Another hunter lifted a club weighted with a round stone and struck Phillip on the side of the head. As Caroline and Miles backed away, Phillip fell hard to the ground and was surrounded by the hunters who drove the butts of their spears down on him to stop him from rising.

Caroline was the first to turn and run back up the hill with Miles close behind her. She heard a grunt and a crash as Miles fell rolling into the brush but didn't stop her headlong flight. She raced for the top of the mesa, muttering a prayer that the field was still open. She had no thought beyond that but fleeing; to put this danger far behind her and find the safety of her own time and place and never, ever leave there again.

There were sounds and barked exchanges of hunters from the brush to either side of her joined by long blasts from horns. They were cutting her off, getting ahead of her. She'd never make the mesa top. Even if she could reach it, the window for the field to be open could have passed by now. She'd be on coverless open grassland with nowhere to hide.

Ducking into some thick underbrush, she followed a cleft in the hillside made by run-off from rainstorms in the past. The gully carried her down the hill but offered concealment behind its high banks to either side. She made herself move slowly and cautiously. Her pursuers grew quiet as well. She could hear them exchanging hushed words, and the brittle snaps of pine twigs reached her ears. They had her trapped and were only being as quiet as they needed to be before the final rush.

With a hollow feeling in the pit of her stomach, Caroline realized that she would not escape.

The hunters had her ringed and were closing in from all sides. Her mouth and throat were painfully dry. She tried to control her breathing to stay quiet as long as she could. She fumbled in a cargo pocket at the front of her vest and pulled out her wave transmitter. Thumbing it on, she tried to enter words into the tiny keyboard with shaking hands.

HUNTING HORNS MUST HIDE

At least, that's what she thought she'd texted. What came through was:

HNTGHRNS MST HDE

The brush around her was parted by spear points, and rough, calloused hands dragged her from her hiding place.

THEY LED HER AND Miles down to the beach, their hands bound with thongs and pulled by leashes tied around their throats. Miles was sobbing and could not stop himself. Caroline was numb with fear and dread. Behind them, two hunters pulled a travois across the sand bearing a cargo of Phillip's head, legs, and arms covered in a swirling haze of flies. They'd left the torso behind. Miles told her later that he witnessed the dismemberment. They held him so he couldn't turn away. Phillip was alive but unconscious as they chopped at him with obsidian head axes. The lead hunter poked the torso that remained with a stick, jabbing at the yellow Batman symbol and speaking in a low voice. None of them would touch the shirt to remove it even when the leader slashed at them with the stick and snarled orders. They finally left it behind.

Batman was bad mojo to them.

At the village, the entire tribe came from their huts and fires to gather around Caroline and Miles. The settlement was a messy expanse of huts that roughly followed the shoreline. It looked like it could house thousands. The squatty hominids cooed in wonder and barked with a sound Caroline later came to recognize as laughter. They poked at their unwilling guests with sticks and fingers, and the children dared one another to rush forward and brush hands across their clothing and skin. The children were shooed away by the adults, and all grew quiet.

The crowd about them parted and a man painted all in white stepped up to them. He wore a tall feather headdress of what looked like goose and heron plumage. It was decorated with stones and shells, and he wore many ropes of necklaces of the same type. Some of the stones were dull yellow. Others had been polished to a sheen.

Gold.

This shaman, as Caroline guessed he was, also wore some amulets crudely hammered into animal shapes from unrefined gold ore.

The shaman waved a rod over them. The rod was capped by a gourd with pebbles within it. It made a rattling sound as he moved it over Caroline and Kemp in complicated ritual gestures. He hummed tunelessly as he did so with eyes pressed shut. He then turned his attention to the travois and its gruesome cargo. Squatting, he reached out and touched the fabric covering Phillip's severed legs. He raised his fingers to his nose and sniffed. He turned to the others and hissed a phrase that drew a gasp of awe from the crowd of squat, naked men and women.

Caroline studied their captors. They looked less than human. Their skulls had a pronounced brow ridge, with disturbingly large eyes set deep over flat noses and obscenely broad mouths lined with pickets of black teeth. Their shoulders were wide, and their spines curved forward. Their feet were longer and narrower than was normal, and their fingers ended in knobbed, calloused tips with thick nailbeds. The ears were smaller and set farther back on the head. She continued to think of them as aborigines, but only because she had no other term for them. They were closer to animals than humans, and she knew she was looking at a vanished race of proto-humans. High-order primates with little shared DNA between themselves and their unlucky visitors.

Standing up, the shaman stiffened his body and pointed his stick at Miles and Caroline and called out a long string of what had to be orders. The pair were dragged up the hill toward the cave opening, where the vile hag that Caroline would name Old Mother waited.

They were shoved and yanked into the dark of the cave, where Old Mother and a dozen or so women of the tribe took over. Caroline was brought to the ground by many small hands. She struggled to rise and was swatted across the face with a stick with enough force to make her vision swim. More weight was brought to bear, and she was pressed to the sand and held still. Old Mother straddled her torso and stared defiantly into Caroline's eyes. She made clucking sounds and reached out a hand. One of Caroline's captors placed a curved flint blade in Old Mother's palm. A skinning knife.

Caroline bucked and writhed but was held firm as Old Mother bent over her and used the knife to cut her clothing away. With sure hands, the ancient bitch sliced away her shirt, t-shirt, pants, and panties. The hiking boots stymied them, so they left them in place for now. Old Mother crouched down by Caroline and explored her mouth with filthy fingers that tasted like ash and rancid fat. The clawed hands worked their way down to painfully squeeze her breasts. She fought hard, but the hands of the women yanked her legs apart, and Old Mother put fingers in Caroline's vagina and rectum. The toothless old woman then sat back to sniff at her hands. She held the hands out, and others leaned forward to sniff and make hushed remarks.

They released Caroline, who leaped up on her feet with hands fisted. The women used growled threats and gestured with stones in their hands to make her back against a wall at the rear of the cave. She stumbled into a heap of objects that clattered under her feet, and the women shrieked in rage and struck at her with fists and stones until she moved to a wall away from their precious pile. She fell on her ass against the rock and looked back to see what was worth getting so damned upset about.

Heaped high in a corner of the cave was a pile of hammered gold plates, tablets, and talismans. The corner was formed by a niche in the stone with a natural shelf of rock upon which sat the crudely hammered figure of a fertility fetish. It was faceless and crouched on stubby, fat legs. The figure had huge orbs representing breasts, as well as a prodigious phallus jutting from its crotch. It had to weigh hundreds of pounds. *The golden penis alone would fund her work for a year, she imagined. At its feet were hundreds, possibly thousands more pounds of objects hammered from soft gold.*

She turned as she heard Miles pleading softly with the women, as though he might reason with them. They repeated the same ritual they'd performed on Caroline, but Miles was a big man and kept throwing them off until Old Mother brought a stone the size of a baking potato down on his head. Miles went still. He either lost consciousness or was afraid to move. Caroline couldn't tell which.

Old Mother sliced off his clothes, leaving the boots as the women weighed down his legs and arms. Much was made of his genitals, and the women hissed and whispered and barked as Old Mother stroked the dazed Miles to an erection. She slapped the reaching hands of the others away with a stream of spitting invective.

The old woman and her entourage turned their attention back to Caroline. They took turns touching her and prodding while Old Mother crushed soft stone mixed with water in a carved wooden bowl using a crude pestle made from a limb bone. The Old Mother slathered Caroline with the lime wash using her calloused hand. She worked the mess into Caroline's hair while the others watched and exchanged whispers and hisses. Old Mother daubed ashes mixed with gobs of her own spit around Caroline's eyes using her thumbs. She draped Caroline with necklaces of bone and beads worked from gold nuggets the size of fingertips.

Old Mother sat back and looked on her work with satisfaction. She touched Caroline's face gently. Caroline stiffened and willed herself not to recoil. For whatever reason, they were honoring her with special treatment. Stockholm Syndrome or not, Caroline was determined not to do anything to piss them off and get her and Miles chopped to bits like poor Phillip.

Miles had his wrists bound behind him and his feet placed on a log, where his ankles were tied with lines run through holes worked in the log. Caroline was bound the same way and left alone as Old Mother and her entourage departed for the daylight, leaving them alone in the golden glow of the fire reflecting off the half-ton of treasure lying ten feet away.

"Miles?" Caroline said in a croak. She worked her mouth and spat, the rank taste of the old crone's fingers still on her tongue.

"Miles, can you hear me?"

Her answer was a wet sobbing. Miles had his head turned away from her.

"We're going to get out of here," Caroline said. "I don't know how or who's coming for us, but I know my brother won't just leave us here. I texted him. He knows our situation."

Miles may have answered her, or maybe it was only a wordless whine.

"Hang on, Miles," she said to him in a voice flat and without a hint of anxiety.

Hang on, Caroline, she thought to herself.

She fought down a shiver.

The next morning, after the disastrous raid by the men sent by Morris Tauber, Old Mother came awake as the shaman strode into the cave.

The ancient crone blocked his path and shrieked at him. He shouted back and gestured and glared at Caroline, sitting helpless at the rear of the cave. His face was dark with rage even under the lime wash. His flesh was spattered with the still-drying blood of his tribesmen. Fresh blood trickled from a jagged cut to the outside of his thigh. The mouth of the cave was crowded with curious tribe members anxious to see this argument. Many of them bore scars and burns.

The shaman tried to get past the old woman time and again, but she struck at him with a stone clenched in her fist. He waved his gourd stick and made dire threats or was perhaps only growling. She kicked ash and sand at him and spat on him over and over. After a long exchange that echoed and re-echoed off the cave wall, the shaman finally retreated, his huge dark eyes boring into Caroline's until he was out of sight.

Old Mother crawled to Caroline on hands and knees and hugged her close. Caroline stiffened. The stinking, greasy witch cooed softly and rocked Caroline back and forth, stroking her hair.

Caroline was safe as long as Old Mother held her as precious, or until the bitch got hungry.

10

THE LAND OF BEER AND PRETZELS

Parviz and Quebat drove Renzi down to the urgent care center in Alamo. He was barely conscious and went easily. His only request was a cigarette, but there were no smokers here.

"You saw Caroline?" Tauber said again as Chaz stripped off the ragged and filthy BDUs and tossed them in a trash can by the row of sinks.

"We saw her," Chaz said. "We couldn't get to her." He reached into a tiled stall and turned on the shower.

"What about Phillip and Miles?" Tauber said, voice rising.

"Look, Doc," Chaz stepped into the stall shower under a near-scalding pins-and-needles stream. "Time is relative, as you kept telling us. I'll tell you the whole damn story in full detail. Now, you can stand there admiring my fine black ass, or you can go fry me up some eggs and sausage and pour me a cold glass of milk as big as my head and give me a fistful of Tylenols, and then I'll answer every one of your questions whether you like the answers or not."

Chaz was wiping yolk from his plate with the corner of an English muffin, and the doc topped off the tumbler of milk. He was in clean, dry jeans and a work shirt, with sandals on his feet. He ached all over and his body was hungry for sleep, but there was no time for pain or rest.

"There are people there, Doc. Nasty little, mean fuckers. They killed the grad student, and we watched them kill Dr. Kemp. But your sister is still alive, and they're treating her like some kind of Disney princess."

He left out the cannibal aspect. No need for the doc to know that. Chaz needed the man focused and not running nightmare scenarios through his mind. Things would happen fast now. It was going to be a busy forty-eight hours.

"Where are Roenbach and Small?" Tauber poured himself some coffee and stirred it. "They're alive and keeping watch," Chaz said. "But all they have is a two-shot pocket pistol, a Buck knife, and my Zippo. I have to get back there as soon as you have the Tube up and running, and I can bring some heavier shit back with me."

"Heavier?"

"Real ordnance, Doc. Not those damn rocket guns. Some real shit. SAWs and M4s and frags and body armor. If we're gonna bring your sister out, we gotta *kill* our way to her."

"But the indigenous population…" Tauber began.

"Fuck 'em."

"But they're an entirely unknown, extinct tribe of humans who arrived on the continent and thrived there tens of millennia before the first known Native Americans crossed the Bering Strait."

"So maybe we're the ones who made them extinct," Chaz said and set the empty tumbler down. "You ever think of that?"

"Still, to exterminate…"

"You starting to lose your enthusiasm here, Doc? Trust me,

one of these little fuckers wouldn't mind exterminating *you*. Now, are you into the game or in the way?"

"Renzi won't be any shape to go with you, not in forty-eight hours."

"I know," Chaz said. He picked up a cell phone and touched the keys. "We have another recruit."

Tauber was still stirring his coffee as Chaz listened to the ring tone.

Six rings. Seven. A click on the other end. "Hammond."

"I'm done here," Lee Hammond said and tossed to the desktop a laminated ID badge with the name Carter, Dolan J. next to an overexposed photo of himself scowling for the camera.

"This is kind of sudden," the blonde behind the desk said. "You've got vacation coming, Dole."

"Got a better offer," Hammond said and pulled off the jacket with the White Horse Security Inc badge sewn on the sleeve. He folded it and put it on the desk by the badge.

"Captain Hodge isn't going to be happy."

"When is Captain Hodge ever happy?"

"What about your benefits?" the blonde said and watched him unbuckle the gun belt around his waist. "Insurance, retirement. You qualify for dental next month."

"Don't need them," Hammond said as he placed the gun belt by the folded jacket. He slipped the Colt Python from the clamshell holster, flipped the cylinder out, and dropped the six fat rounds into his palm. He placed the rounds atop the folded jacket. "Company's ammo. The Colt's mine."

"We're gonna miss you, Dole," the blonde said and came around the desk.

"Yeah," he said and pulled his own leather jacket from a steel rack bolted on the office wall.

"We were just getting to know each other," she said and leaned back on the desk, long legs crossed, skirt riding up to heaven. She tilted her head and smiled crookedly.

"Darling," Hammond said as he turned and opened the office door. "I think you know just about everything there is to know about me."

———

Chaz stepped off the jet to find Hammond waiting for him on the tarmac, standing by a battered Jeep Cherokee spotted with primer. It was a small county airport outside Rexford, Idaho, one strip, one hangar, nothing but flat fields of soybeans all around, and the Rockies way off on the horizon. The crew deplaned and went into the airport's mini-lounge to await Chaz's return.

Chaz threw a Nike bag into the rear seat of the Jeep and Hammond drove them away on a two-lane blacktop that ran straight as a string through miles of soy.

"You leave a job for this?" Chaz said after a while.

"Security," Hammond said. "A wind farm."

"They need that much security?"

"Naw. The crazies are only pissed at the nuke plants. Mostly shooing away campers."

"So, it was quiet then?"

"Not really," Hammond said, eyes on the road. "Those windmills are noisy as hell."

Hammond pulled onto the gravel lot of a mom-and-pop truck stop off 20 and they found a booth.

"You need some heavy ordnance, bro," Hammond said after the waitress left coffee and a carafe.

"And your services, if you're up for it," Chaz said.

"Domestic or foreign?" Hammond said. "That make a difference?"

"Not for the kind of money you're talking about.

It's two days, and you never leave the country," Chaz said. "And you're on a tight schedule."

"We need to be guns-up and on post in thirty-six hours."

"Let's go shopping." Hammond whistled for the waitress and made a circle motion over the coffee carafe. "We need this to go, darling."

The strip mall sat as dead as an ancient burial ground at the back of an acre of cracked asphalt. Three cars sat at a faded old KFC by the road. There was a boarded-up Olive Garden. The strip of stores was anchored by a shut-down discount store on one end and a shut-down supermarket on the other. The only occupied stores were a Chinese take-out and a place called simply Guns/Pawn that sat next to the shuttered Sav-A-Lot Market.

"You vouch for this guy?" Chaz said.

"I dealt with him a few times," Hammond said. "He didn't screw me over, and he doesn't talk."

"It's just, I mean, he's set up shop in a strip mall."

"Hiding in plain sight."

"I guess," Chaz said. They drove past empty shopping cart corrals.

"You need this stuff in a hurry," Hammond said. "That doesn't leave a lot of options. Hurry means risk, and hurry means money. Live with it, Raleigh."

Hammond pulled around the back and parked by a military-model Hummer finished in real tree camo. He knocked at the heavy metal door set in the back wall. Chaz held the Nike bag under his arm.

The rusting door creaked open to reveal a metal bar-lock and slap bolts top and bottom. The wall around it would come down before this door ever fell. A heavyset guy with biker tats met them with an open smile. He had an automatic in a pancake holster in the shadow of his spreading gut. His t-shirt read TAX THIS! with an arrow pointing toward his crotch.

"Meet Wall," Hammond said. Wall held a hand out.

"You are?" Wall smiled, revealing two missing upper front teeth. The butt of an unfiltered Camel dangled from his lip.

"Mister Cash," Chaz said.

Wall laughed with a wet rumble deep in his chest. Emphysema or worse.

"Well, shit. You're *always* welcome, Mister Cash!" He pulled the door aside and let them by.

The back room was typical pawn. Some dirt bikes. Shelves of appliances and musical instruments. Chaz glanced through the door to the front room, where there were rows of lighted show counters loaded with watches, rings, necklaces, handguns, and knives. The walls were lined with rifles and shotguns chained into racks. The front windows and door had heavy iron bars set in them. A rail-thin woman in a t-shirt and jeans sat smoking in a register cage, watching a small TV monitor. She wore a snubby revolver in a clip-on holster in the waistband of her jeans at the small of her back.

"Goin' in the back, Jolinda," Wall called.

"Uh-huh," she sang back, never taking her eyes from the TV. One of those courtroom shows where low-rent dickheads made fools of themselves in front of a studio audience, arguing over shit only they cared about.

Wall led them to where an area rug embroidered with a portrait of Bruce Lee posed to whup ass hung from a line. Wall pulled the rug aside to reveal a concealed doorway chipped out of the cinderblock firewall. He worked the locks with a big ring of keys chained to his belt and swung the door in. A fluorescent light flickered on, and they were in the large walk-in freezer of the shuttered supermarket next door. The door leading out to the market's stockroom was blocked by a pair of heavy wooden bars chained in place.

"I own the whole strip," Wall said with a damp chuckle. "'Cept the Chinese place. That dude is a stone holdout."

Instead of sides of beef and boxes of frozen poultry, the freezer contained crates piled high on pallets in even rows. There was several million dollars in government ordnance here, American and foreign. High-end stuff. The room smelled of Cosmoline and gun oil. Smelt like home.

"Hammond said you were looking to outfit four men for a long-range op?" Wall leaned back on a stack of crates and lit a new Camel with the old one.

"Got a grocery list," Chaz said. "I want four M4s. Bushmaster frames if you have 'em. Five thousand rounds of .223.

"In mags or cartons?"

"Cartons. We'll load our own mags. And we'll need 30-round mags. Eighty of them, minimum."

Wall stuck out his lower lip and nodded. "Got drum mags if you want 'em."

"Drums aren't worth shit."

"No problem. What else?"

"A SAW and a thousand rounds. A dozen box mags. Spare barrel. Make it two spare barrels."

"I got an FN Minimi in primo. Got a Chinese type 88 but I'm guessing you're not interested in economizing."

"You're right," Chaz nodded. "It's our asses on the line. I want reliable. We'll take the Minimi."

"Got you covered. What else is on that list?"

"Frags. HE. Some smoke grenades. Four sets of body armor. And NODs."

"You need sidearms?" Wall began walking through the rows of crates. "Got some sweet Sigs."

"We're covered on that. We have a long gun and shotguns. From you, we need the government-issue stuff."

"How about a Ma Deuce?" Wall patted a wooden crate eight feet in length stenciled M-2, .50 CAL.

Chaz and Hammond exchanged a look that set Wall on a bout of laughing that turned to a spasm of coughing that almost brought the old biker to his knees.

An hour later they were wheels up, the Gulfstream a ton heavier and Chaz's Nike bag a quarter-million lighter. They dropped down at a private field just west of Coyote Springs ninety minutes later and drove the two hours to the compound pulling a rusting horse trailer behind the doc's Land Rover. Just two cowboys headed home through the high country.

11

CAMP NOWHEN

The edge of the escarpment jutted well clear of the lip of the mesa and had a good view of the skinnies' village below. It formed a natural redoubt, surrounded on three sides by steep walls that would make for a difficult approach. A game trail wound down from behind the position, concealed by brush and berry bushes on either side. Access back to the field site was an easy, level thirty minute hike to the east. It was the perfect hide and perfect observation post.

Dwayne glassed the village and, for the hundredth time, cursed the weak ten-power binoculars they'd packed along. But they brought him close enough to see some of the activity below. The day was clear and visibility good. Many of the huts were just black stains on the sand now. Others were knocked flat by concussion from the satchel charges. The skinnies were stripping the burnt hooches for useable materials. The women and children of the tribe carried scorched logs and branches and placed them in a pile either for burning or to build new huts.

The males had already gathered up the dead in the day and a half it took Dwayne and Jimbo to make their way around the lake and up to this vantage point. Dwayne could see no wounded, and that meant that anyone who survived the fight with injuries had been executed or left to bleed out. Dwayne counted forty-six bodies laid out in the sand, and the men worked over them as though they were game. He recognized the motions, even if he could see little detail. Each corpse was strung up on a gibbet by the ankles to empty their veins. They were gutting the corpses and skinning them before carving meat from the bones. The skins were stretched on a line like some horrible load of laundry strung out to dry. The guts and bones were left in a pile for the dogs to fight over. Some of the innards, hearts and livers probably, were thrown into baskets woven from reeds and carried away by the women. A toddler no more than three rushed up and snatched what had to be a liver from a basket and evaded swats from the men. The little one ran off to gnaw at the dripping slab in the shelter of a ruined hut like it was a slice of birthday cake.

Dwayne had seen his share of horrors but he had to move the lenses away from that sight.

The rockface above the cave was speckled with the black shapes of carrion birds, big turkey buzzards squatting on every available rock and ledge. More and more arrived throughout the day. Now and then one of the big-winged birds would dare to swoop down and snatch a discarded bit of flesh from the pile. Children of the tribe would laugh and throw rocks at the vultures as they soared back up the cliff with long strings of flesh dangling from their beaks.

The hide was a good four hundred yards from and above the village, but the stink of that butcher's heap still reached him. Dwayne couldn't see but he could imagine the clouds of flies and God knew what other prehistoric pests that were probably hovering over the camp.

He returned the binoculars to his main area of attention, the cave opening. Caroline was not visible. If she lived, they were keeping her inside the cave. The only skinnies allowed entry were women who carried meat and water inside but did not stay.

The dude painted all in white with the wild headdress, the one who lorded over Kemp's execution, was never far from the cave opening but did not enter. He was a chief or witch doctor. No way to be sure. Once, a bent-over old woman came from the cave and threw rocks at him, and he moved away. Dwayne had no idea what any of that meant but had a gut feeling it was a good thing.

And good things had a way of coming to an end.

Dwayne wanted to get closer, but there was no safe or defensible location nearer the village. And the settlement was more extensive than they realized the night they showed up. It stretched to the west along the beach far from the bonfire that they had incorrectly assumed was at the center of the village. The huts around the black fire pit were burnt or blown down but there were many more still intact in a sprawling section of the village that ran all the way to the opposite wall of the bowl.

He figured there were four hundred adult males minimum in camp, along with three or four times that many women and kids who would fight as well. He guessed that was a complete count since there was no need for any hunting parties to be out with all the available meat around. It didn't appear they'd sent anyone out to look for the strangers who attacked them. But there was no way to be sure of that. Maybe he was right and the skinnies assumed the Rangers had drowned. If they couldn't swim themselves, they'd naturally think that the strange visitors could not either.

The Rangers had underestimated the skinnies in their first encounter by assuming they'd scatter at the first blast. Judging from the piles of tusks, the skinnies hunted the big mastodons that almost made Dwayne and the others lose their mud. The skinnies might be cruel, man-eating assholes, but what they *weren't* was cowards. They had the reckless courage of mad dogs. It was going to be a fight to get Caroline out of the cave and away.

A low whistle from the brush came behind him. Dwayne

dropped the binoculars and picked up one of the spears he made earlier in the morning. Just straight tree limbs sharpened on one end with the clasp knife.

Jimbo parted the branches of the scrub pine and headed toward Dwayne, his approach concealed from below by the lip of the escarpment. He carried a crude bow made from bundled reeds bound together with vines and a boot lace for a string. Six unfletched arrows, made with seasoned wood that Jimbo found in a dead patch of berry bushes were wrapped in an improvised quiver fashioned from a shirt sleeve. They'd work well enough close in.

"Any action?" Jimbo knelt and pulled out some long black feathers from inside his shirt. He was barefoot. He gave up his boots to Renzi and Dwayne wore the other surviving pair. No problem. He'd spent half his life on the reservation shoeless.

"No sign of Caroline Tauber," Dwayne said. "But the old witch is keeping the men out of the cave. I take that as a positive sign. What do you think?"

"You asking me that as a pesky redskin? You think I have some aboriginal wisdom to impart?"

"I'm asking for a guess, dickhead."

"Beats the shit outta me, paleface. Could be the women want to eat her and the men want to fuck her, and the women are in there marinating her right now."

"Thanks for that sunny prognosis. What's going on up at the insertion site?"

"The field's not open," Jimbo said and sat cross-legged. "But I set up a sign using rocks to point them to our camp." He worked at splitting the feathers down the center of their quills using the point of his clasp knife.

"No way of knowing how long we have to wait," Dwayne said and rolled on his belly to return to his vigil.

"Think Hammond will come along?"

"Chaz and a buttload of cash can be pretty persuasive. If Chaz can find him."

"Yeah," Jimbo began binding a six-inch length of feather to the shaft of one of the arrows with a length of thread stripped from his shirt. He wound it round and round with infinite patience.

Dwayne raised the binoculars and eyed the white-painted chief. He was easy to pick out from the others even at a distance. The chief sat watching the cave opening from the shade of an outcropping. He was fixated on the cave every bit as much as Dwayne was.

"What if they don't come?" Jimbo said after a while. "What if something goes wrong on the other end?"

"Wrong like what?"

Jimbo chuckled. One arrow was fletched, and he set it aside and picked up another.

"Anything could go wrong, Dwayne. That reactor breaks down. The coil breaks. Computer failure. The whole damned thing could just blow up. Maybe the feds show up asking questions about why two Iranian illegals are running an unauthorized nuke plant."

"So, we stay here and make the best of it," Dwayne said. The chief was up and pacing, walking halfway to the cave mouth, then walking back to his shady spot.

"We don't even know if a return trip is possible. Ever think of that? Maybe Chaz and Renzi vanished into the universe in a billion pieces."

"We stay here, Jimbo."

"The rest of our lives?"

"Yeah. Forever till the day we die. Could you deal with that?"

"Sure. Might make for a hell of a life. Plenty of game. Fresh air and good water. No taxes and nowhere I need to be."

"Spoken like a true pesky redskin." Dwayne watched the white-painted chief who laid back in the shade but raised himself up on an elbow to keep watch on the cave.

"Back to my roots. I could even take a squaw."

Dwayne lowered the binoculars and turned back to Jimbo, working at his arrows.

"Seriously?"

"Sure," Jimbo said, inspecting the fletching on a second arrow. "Clean one of them up, and they might look pretty good after a month or two."

"Even with the sharpened teeth?"

"That might be a problem, bro."

Dwayne snorted and turned back to glass the village. The lime-washed chief wasn't under the outcropping. He swept left and right. No chief. Where did he go? Did he get into the cave while Dwayne was turned away?

No, there he was, speaking and gesturing to the males busy rendering the bodies. A few stopped their work to listen. Two of the larger males came over and shoved the smaller man away; not buying his rap. These guys were war chiefs or hunting chiefs. Alpha males. Taller and more muscled than the others. Dwayne named them Fred and Barney. They gestured and barked at the others who turned away to continue their grisly labors. The little white-washed man kicked sand at them and stormed off waving his hands above his head. He went back and sat cross-legged in front of the cave in a clear sulk.

So, Whitey wasn't a chief. The white-painted skinny had to be a shaman or priest, and one without much power to command. Maybe the red-painted bastard Jimbo nailed with a headshot two nights ago was the chief, and now the skinnies were leaderless except for Fred and Barney. Or maybe the old lady in the cave called the shots. Dwayne was still going to keep an eye on the lime-washed guy.

"You know," Jimbo said as he finished fletching the last arrow. "There is one eligible female here I wouldn't mind hooking up with."

Dwayne turned back to regard him with narrowed eyes.

"But I have a strong feeling she's spoken for." Jimbo looked up with a disarming smile.

That night, they ate rabbit that Jimbo snared for dinner. Big jackrabbits. Everything was bigger here except the people. Throughout the afternoon, they saw evidence of that. Butterflies the size of birds skimmed flowers growing in a clearing. Moose easily ten feet at the shoulder stood munching cattails in the shallows along the shore.

On the hike around the lake to their current position, they crossed a causeway between the sea and a small lake. It wasn't a natural formation but a dam made of mud packed between logs. Moving under the still water along the causeway, they could see dark shapes rippling the surface; beavers the size of black bears. Jimbo wondered what size bears were in this country and Dwayne said he'd rather not find out.

Jimbo cooked the pair of rabbits in a pit fire.

He coated them with mud he scooped from around a spring they were using for water and they baked inside the mud, buried in the embers of the pit, so there was no open flame and little smoke. He packed the rabbits with wild onion and asparagus. Dessert was salmonberries.

They wouldn't starve.

There was no big bonfire in the village that night. That must have been a ceremonial thing for feasting on Dr. Kemp. Instead, there were dozens of smaller cook fires w strips of their neighbors hung from spits over the flames. That left the area in front of the cave in shifting shadow. Dwayne couldn't be certain of who was going in or out of there in the dark. NOD gear would be a godsend right now. And if Jimbo was right. Those eyes on the skinnies meant they had an advantage in the dark. The bigger the eyes, the more light they let in.

"I don't want to wait anymore," Dwayne said. "I want to go down there tonight and get her out."

"Chaz could be back tomorrow," Jimbo said. He was making more arrows for his quiver. He had twenty or more now.

"Or next week. Or never. And the situation is not improving down there. That witch doctor or shaman or whatever wants in that cave and the old lady has to sleep sometime."

"Any idea what he wants?" Jimbo said. "Maybe he's horny."

"I don't think so," Dwayne said. "If that were true, the rest would be trying to get in, too. I think the little witch doctor lost face or mojo. Eating Kemp might have been a power thing, some kind of blood magic. When we showed up, it all went wrong. The witch doctor looks weak now."

"You've been thinking about this," Jimbo said.

"All fucking day. It makes sense, right?"

"Well, we tried rushing them, and that went south. Maybe a quarterback sneak. When do we leave?"

Dwayne looked into the sky. There was a sliver of moon showing and a bank of heavy clouds moving in over the sea.

"When the weather moves over the moon we start down," he said.

"Maybe while we're down there, we can pick up a date for me." Jimbo grinned.

12

STANDARD TIME

D r. Morris Tauber sat at the kitchen table in the living quarters and stared without really seeing anything at the little TV set on the table. The sound was turned down to a whisper. It was a rerun of some kind of cop show. From the eighties, if the haircuts were any indication.

Parviz entered from the outside. He wore a parka and sweater. It got close to freezing here at night, and he'd been checking connections around the tower.

"We are good for going in the morning," Parviz said. "Structure is sound, and Quebat checked levels on the reactor. It will even be especially dry tomorrow. Most optimum of conditions, are they not?"

Tauber made a noise rather than a spoken answer.

"You are sick, Doctor?" Parviz peeled off the parka. His sweater was garish, decorated with reindeer and snowflakes. It usually made Tauber laugh, the juxtaposition of cultures. It was hard to picture the Iranian at a ski lodge.

"Do you think the physical laws of the universe are immutable?" Tauber asked and looked up to meet Parviz's eyes.

"They are the laws," Parviz answered. "But only as we understand them."

"Right." Tauber nodded. He swallowed. "Our understanding is limited."

"Theoretical," Parviz added helpfully. "Yes," Tauber said and turned his gaze back to the TV where a car chase down a dusty LA street was grinding on.

"You are thinking of your sister," Parviz said and opened the refrigerator. "Of what we found."

"It's her," Tauber said. "She died before she was born. She got that molar crown from our family dentist. There's no changing that."

"You cannot know that," Parviz said and set two bottles of hard lemonade on the table.

"It's done. It can't change, Parviz."

"That is such empirical bullshit, it is. Everything we have done is change. All change. We send your sister and the others back where they should never have been. Just stepping through the field made changes. Sending these men back with their guns changed even more. Tomorrow we send men back again, and even more changes will be made."

"That was a bullet hole in her skull," Tauber said and shook his head as Parviz popped a bottle and held it to him. "It came from one of the men I sent back."

"So, will you not send them tomorrow?" Parviz took a sip from his bottle and licked his lips.

"I have to," Tauber said. "Or maybe I can't. I don't know. I don't know if anything I do will help or hurt Caroline or if it's too late for anything and all of this was decided all those years ago."

"If done is done then you can't hurt her anymore," Parviz said. "And this way you will know what happened. In any case, it is written. We see the changes we made as new and very surprising.

But God knows all and has put in place these events long before we became a part of them."

"You're going to the Quran on me?" Tauber said. "The same book that condemns you and Quebat to death for being who you are?"

"The word of the Prophet is up to the believer," Parviz said. "I take what I want from the early verses. It is just like any other faith. I cannot walk away because some men choose different passages to guide them."

Tauber took the bottle and tipped it back, half emptying the frosted bottle in three gulps.

"And you will know, in any case, it is the end of the bastards who brought you this pain," Parviz said.

"Do you mean the aborigines or Roenbach's men?" Tauber said.

"Does it matter?"

Tauber drained the bottle.

"That's fucked up. "Hammond spat on the floor in front of the Tauber Tube. They were powering it up in prep for the trip tomorrow. The coils were already frosting over.

"It's all true," Chaz said. "Fucked up," Hammond said.

"Have I ever lied to you?" Chaz said. "Bangkok," Hammond said without turning.

"I told you then I didn't know that hooker was a dude."

"Only thing that makes me believe you is that cash you're handing around. *That* I believe in."

"Dr. Tauber explained—"

"Dr. Tauber does not inspire confidence," Hammond cut him off. "And those two Hadji fruitloops don't help his case. But you're no bullshitter, and I already got plans for my pay."

"There's another upside," Chaz said. "We can go do a full recon on the ground. The terrain is the same, except for differences I can point out. But the elevations and approaches to the skinny village are basically just like what we experienced."

"Let's go take a look," Hammond said.

On foot, they followed new 4x4 tracks all the way down off the mesa. It had to be the doc's Land Rover that made them and they couldn't be more than a week old. They were able to follow the tracks right to the opening of the cave, where tires marks crisscrossed around piles of freshly excavated earth.

While Hammond surveyed the ground they'd be fighting over, Chaz crouched to enter the cave. The floor level had been scraped lower by ten feet or more. It went back a good fifty feet and ended where some bones had been dug up in a far corner. He couldn't see much in the gloom. The desert sunlight didn't penetrate far.

He could pick out ribs and some long bones, and the sight made him shake off a chill. This was someone's grave. Was this the history of the firefight they'd be walking into tomorrow? Was he looking at all that remained of his own future buried all this time ago in a cave, untouched for thousands of years?

Chaz backed out of the cave. Shit like that could test your head. Or break it. He rejoined Hammond who was walking back to the cave from what was the receding shoreline of the ancient lake. He told himself not to mention the bones to Lee.

"So, we're good?"

"Yeah, we're good," Hammond said. "But I only have one question for the doc."

"We'll go ask him right now," Chaz said. "What's the question?"

"Can we make two trips through this thing at one go?"

———

"Two trips?" asked Tauber.

Chaz and Hammond stood before the coil in full gear the following morning. Dark forest camo BDUs, ballcaps, tactical gloves, body armor, ammo packs, rifle, frags, HE grenades, sidearms, and combat knives. Hammond had a Benelli combat shotgun strapped to his pack with Velcro strips and an ammo belt with its loops packed with fat buckshot and flechette rounds. The Tube was near maximum. It was giving off vapor. Clumps of frost dripped from it to make a puddle on the floor.

"We got that big ass fifty-cal to hump through," Hammond gestured to the massive heavy machine gun resting on a tripod next to piles of steel ammo boxes and equipment totes. "And all the extra ammo and gear."

"I suppose there's no reason," Tauber eyed the pile of ordnance with misgiving. "But the physical effects of multiple transfers might be unpleasant."

"Yeah." Chaz nodded. "The first trip through kicks your ass."

"Can't be helped. We need the Ma Deuce."

"May I ask why?" Tauber said.

"That's our back door," Hammond gestured to the Tube. "We need to cover it as we fall back."

"You'll bring everything back with you?" Tauber said. "And every*one*?"

"We'll do our best, Doc," Chaz said.

"And if we can't pack the gear back, we know where it is, right?" Hammond said. "We just go out and dig up what's left of it, and no one's the wiser."

"Yes," Tauber said in a low voice. "Theoretically, anyway."

ONE NIGHT IN BEDROCK

Athick, drifting funk lay over the skinnies' village. Smoke from smoldering fires left untended was heavy on the ground. There was a greasy tang to it, like ribs left too long on the grill.

The skinnies slept where they fell, sated and logy after a feast on the flesh of their own villagers. Even the dogs were passed out, gorged on tripe. A fresh stack of bones lay by the makeshift abattoir. There were long strips of meat strung up out of reach of the dogs, jerky for later. Skins were stretched on lines. The victims were expertly flayed. The translucent leather of their hides looked like kites made of parchment, the forms of humans grotesquely defined. The cut-out eyes and mouths were frozen in an eternal expression of woe. Fat still dripped from the skins that were left to be scraped the following morning.

Heavy cloud cover hid the sliver of the moon from view. The only available light was a reddish glow of fires through the suffocating haze that clung around the huts.

Dwayne moved out of the deeper shadows of the trees with a spear in his fists. He'd hardened the point by searing it in the embers of Jimbo's cookfire. Twenty paces behind, Jimbo covered the drag with an arrow ready in his bow and a quiver filled with twenty more shafts slung from his belt. They'd painted their hands and faces and any other exposed skin black with ash from their fire.

They used the rubbish piles of bones and the tanning racks for cover to move closer to the cave mouth. The last couple hundred feet or so was wide open with no cover. Only luck would carry them over that ground without being seen by a skinny or one of their mutts.

Dwayne crouched by a bone pile. It was swarming with ants and beetles. He looked down to see the skull of what looked like a five-year-old child, its face still in place on the front of the white bone shell and staring from eyeless sockets. The kids were just as murderous as their parents, and he recalled the storm of stones flung at them with punishing accuracy by little bastards just like this one. But still; it was a child, one of their own. And they'd skinned and fed on it.

Lying low and motionless and feeling insects crawling over his exposed flesh, Dwayne peered around the pile. The white-painted witch doctor was nowhere to be seen. Maybe he'd given up his stakeout of the cave. He might be in the village sleeping it off, his belly jammed with meat. Or he could just as well be keeping a vigil from concealment.

A bright, flickering glow came from within the cave. It would throw Dwayne into silhouette as he moved closer and throw his shadow down the incline and over the huts.

He turned back to where he knew Jimbo was kneeling, unseen, in the dark behind him.

"Fuck it," he hissed. "Goin' in."

"All the way," came a hushed reply from the dark.

Caroline Tauber was aching over every inch of her body. She

shifted to find a comfortable position, but only found new agonies. Her fingers were numb and her legs tingly where they were bound to the heavy timber. Her ass ached from hours of pressing on the hard cave floor, and her skin itched fiercely from the lime drying on every inch of her body in the stifling cave.

Old Mother slept fitfully by the fire and, as exhausted as she was, Caroline could not join her. Sleep wouldn't come, and when it did, she awakened seconds later from either physical discomfort or flashes of memory. Phillip screaming as they held him down, the horrible gurgling sound as the aborigine brought the heavy ax down again and again, Kemp's keening pleas for mercy, the probing hands of the gaggle of crones, the expression of fierce rage on the face of the little shaman.

She was weak from hunger, and certainly severely dehydrated. Old Mother offered her strips of rare meat dripping with grease, and she turned her head from it. She'd never be that hungry. At least, she *told* herself that. The only water she had was from a gourd ladle offered by Old Mother. It was brackish and smelled musty, but it cooled her throat.

Back in college at Chicago, she'd dated a cute anthropology major and read some books he recommended. She knew that this was a typical primitive Neolithic culture, a matriarchal society run by a head female who held mystic powers over the tribe. There would be hunting chiefs and war chiefs but for anything beyond that Old Mother called the shots. The world as it was when the chicks were in charge. The arrival of Caroline and the others was seen as Something Big, and so she was placed under the care of the matriarch. Phillip and Miles were just meat.

So what made Caroline special beyond her gender? What were they saving her for? Possibly a harvest festival or, she looked at the grotesque golden fertility statue and shuddered, a fertility rite. Was she to be a holiday meal, or married off to a tribe member?

She contemplated those unpleasant possibilities as she gazed into the flickering fire and, without expecting to, dropped into a deep sleep.

Caroline awakened to find a hand pressed tight to her mouth and another clamped to the back of her head.

A hunched figure blocked the light from the guttering fire.

"Caroline Tauber," the figure said in an urgent whisper. "I am here to get you out of here. Your brother—"

She didn't hear any more because, over the whispering man's shoulder, she saw Old Mother stirring by the fire.

Caroline bit down hard on the man's hand—it tasted like ashes and grease—and he jerked it away suddenly.

"Behind you!" she called.

The man turned in time to see Old Mother rising from her resting spot to stare at him with disbelieving eyes. Her mouth opened, and a cry began to well up from somewhere inside her. He released Caroline and sprang across the cave to deliver a punch to Old Mother's face that dropped her back on her ass, where she began a wailing that echoed and re-echoed off the cave's walls.

He moved to grab her, and the old bitch spider-walked away on heels and palms toward the cave opening, growling like a cat. She picked up a rock as she scuttled away. Dwayne struck his head a glancing blow on the ceiling of the cave rushing in pursuit.

Old Mother was up on her feet and flung the stone, striking him hard in the chest. He grunted and moved after her. She backed almost to the cave opening on the way to rouse the whole village when her feet were suddenly yanked off the cave floor and an arm drawn under her chin in an expert chokehold. She goggled and stretched her lips wide over her few remaining teeth, but no sound escaped. Her struggling slowed and then stopped, and her body went limp.

Jimbo carried her into the cave and dropped her still form to the dirt.

"Move your ass, Dwayne," he said. "The skinnies are making noise moving around down there."

Dwayne bent down by Caroline and began sawing with a long-bladed knife at the leather thongs that bound her to the imprisoning log.

"Get outside and work that bow like a good Indian," Dwayne grunted as he cut her bonds. Jimbo ducked out of the cave and into the dark.

The man named Dwayne cut the thongs at Caroline's wrist, and she looked at him like he was something from a dream.

"Can you stand?" he demanded as he kicked dirt over the fire and plunged the cave into blackness.

"I can run the mile in three minutes if you have someplace to run to," she said and stood and rubbed her wrists. Her hands were pins and needles and ached as blood rushed back into them.

"You'll stay here until I'm sure we have a clear route," he said.

"But—" she began.

"Reach out your hand," the man said. Her eyes were adjusting, and she could see his silhouette in the hazy moonlight from outside.

She stretched her hand out, and he took it in one of his own. He pressed something rounded and metallic into her palm.

"This is a two-shot derringer," he said in a slow instructive tone. "No safety. Pull the trigger and barrel one fires. Pull again and fire one last time. It's the best I can do."

She understood and took the derringer in both hands, feeling the smooth plastic grip and the cold steel of the frame and barrels. One way or another, she had a way out.

"Watch the trigger. It's sensitive. You understand me?"

"Yes," she croaked. Her throat was suddenly dry.

He exited the cave and left her there in the deep dark with raspy breathing coming from Old Mother sprawled unmoving against the wall.

The kids and dogs were the first to arrive. The old hag's howling was enough to rouse some of the camp out of their slumber. The dogs yapped and growled, and the kids began lobbing rocks like the first day of Little League. Dwayne was forced back into the cave mouth. Jimbo took shelter under an overhang of rock that ran along one side of the cliff face. It formed a natural bunker.

Dwayne gripped his spear and weighed their shrinking options. They could only hold the cave opening for so long. The constant storm of stones would keep them pinned down here. The brats didn't even need to be accurate, the sheer number of missiles made leaving the cave an unforgiving choice. They fell like hail, thudding to the sand and shattering on the cliff face. And a few of the little bastards had an arm on them. The bruises on Dwayne's legs and arms multiplied. A blow to the head or an arm or leg bone broken and he'd drop. Then the dogs would rush in.

He was almost glad when Fred and Barney burst through the mob of kids, leading some of the other skinny males behind them. The war chiefs held stout clubs with sharpened flint heads and swung them at the kids and dogs to disperse them. An ax blade neatly beheaded one of the mongrels, and it lay twitching as its lifeblood sprayed out.

The grown-ups were here now, and if there was any killing to be done, it would be them doing it. For now, the rock-throwing was on hold.

Dwayne stepped from the cave to meet the challenge. Fred and Barney rushed forward to flank him left and right. Barney straightened up to stare at the thin shaft that suddenly appeared in his chest. It was buried up to its black feathers between two ribs. He staggered a few more paces before falling to his knees, pink foam spraying from his lips. Jimbo sent a second arrow through the eye socket of another male, forcing the rest of the pack to slow their progress forward.

Fred kept coming, unaware that his partner lay dead on the shale behind him. He swung the war club wildly, and Dwayne ducked aside. The little man was strong out of all proportion to his size and put everything behind the swing.

His momentum carried him stumbling past Dwayne, who turned and jabbed with his spear. Fred took two inches of the fire-hardened point in the small of the back. He shrugged free with a deep grunt. The wound torn in his flank was bleeding freely. Dwayne stepped back and thrust out the spear again, going for the eyes to keep his opponent at a distance.

The white-painted shaman muscled his way through the packed mob of skinnies. He began haranguing the clutch of armed males who backed away farther as two more arrows came out of the dark. One took a skinny through the throat, and he kicked and clawed in the sand, choking out gouts of blood. The other arrow buried deep in the guts of a male and he went to his knees, shrieking in pain through clenched teeth.

The shaman gestured and shoved and barked to get the warriors moving, but their gaze was fixed on their dying tribemates. They jabbered defiance at the shaman. He spat at them and threw handfuls of dirt in an effort to get them worked up.

Fred lumbered forward, swinging the war club back and forth to try and knock Dwayne's spear aside. Dwayne kept himself between the cave opening and the growing mob of skinnies arrayed in a rough half-circle between the cave and the huts.

Jimbo was down to six arrows and wanted to plant them where they'd do the most good. He was judging the mood of the restless males to choose his next target. The shaman was working the crowd to gin them up. Whatever he was screaming at them was starting to work. Jimbo was reminded of a jump instructor at Fort Benning; a pint-sized little runt with a voice that could be heard clearly even at the top of the jump towers. You'd do whatever he said just so he'd shut the hell up.

Jimbo stood up from behind his rock shelter and pulled back on the string. The reed bow strained under the pressure. Jimbo laced the point of the arrow squarely on the shaman's center mass. He let the shaft fly just as a jabbering skinny stepped in the path. The skinny took the arrow through the temple and crashed back into the shaman, knocking them both to the ground.

For some reason, this inspired two skinnies to bolt from the crowd to make a rush at Dwayne. Jimbo nailed one through the side just under the armpit. The skinny stumbled and dropped, awkwardly pulling at the shaft buried in his lungs. A second shaft went deep into the upper thigh of the other local hero, but it didn't slow the guy down at all. He came on for Dwayne's unprotected back.

Dwayne was pinned from behind by powerful arms that were trying to drag him to his knees. His arms were pressed to his side. The skinny with the arrow through his thigh was riding Dwayne in a piggyback.

Fred bounded forward with a holler and swinging the club over his head in wide circles. The blade cut through the air with a thrumming sound. Dwayne gave in to the downward pressure of his rider and crashed with his full weight on the skinny who was gripping him from behind. He drove the skinny hard to the ground and threw himself to one side.

The skinny was gasping to refill his lungs but would not loosen his hold and rode atop Dwayne's back. He didn't release his grip until a poorly aimed swing from Fred took the top of his skull off. The grappler let go and fell to the sand, brains slopping from the disastrous wound that opened his head from the brow line up.

Dwayne freed himself from the twitching skinny and got to

his feet. He still had the spear in his hands and sprang forward as Fred drew the club back for a backhand blow. With all his weight behind the point, Dwayne rammed the spear hard into the solar plexus of the attacker. Fred made a sound like a deep cough as his forward rush impaled him on the point and drove it out his back next to his spine.

It was a mortal wound, but the war chief wasn't ready to die yet and continued swinging for Dwayne's head. Dwayne was staring in disbelief at the ferocious little skinny, who was actually forcing the spear deeper into his chest to get within striking distance of his enemy. With a mad glint out of his eyes and foam flying from his mouth, he kept swinging away. Before he could release the spear shaft, the flat of the ax blade took Dwayne in the side of the head. It was a glancing blow that jarred him. He stumbled and let go of the spear.

That was all the encouragement the rest of the skinnies needed, and they sprinted forward with a roar of triumph exploding from them as though from a single throat. Three spun to the sand with shafts in them, but their comrades trampled the falling bodies to race for Dwayne. The shower of stones picked up again and a fist-sized rock slammed into Dwayne's forehead. He fell back.

He felt fists and clawing hands. Animal growls and the laughter of children filled his ears as the darkness closed.

14

RUNNING LATE

A cab marked Alamo Taxi Service pulled into the compound in a spreading cloud of dust. The rear door flew open, and Renzi ran from it even as the cab brodied to a stop. The driver burst from the cab to chase after him. Renzi could feel the frisson of static still hanging in the air.

"When did they leave?" Renzi demanded as he trotted into the Tube control room.

Tauber turned from his computer array in surprise at the sudden arrival. Renzi was wearing hospital scrubs and docksiders. He had a large patch of his hair shaved off the back of his skull and an angry line of fresh sutures visible there stained with Betadine.

"Ten minutes, a little more," Tauber said. "Pay for the cab!" Renzi called, and ran into the cold cloud of mist falling away from the Tube and was gone. Tauber stared after him and was startled by a strange voice behind him.

A red-faced man in a guayabera shirt, Bermuda shorts and sandals stood behind Tauber looking around.

"Where's the guy I drove up here?" the red-faced man said. "I saw him run in here."

"Um, can I help?" Tauber said.

"He told me he'd pay cash," the red-faced man said. "Both ways. That's three hundred bucks. And he took my Marlboros!"

"I don't have that on me," Tauber said. "You'll have to wait twenty minutes until this shuts down."

"The meter's running, amigo. Double fare, remember?"

"If you take a seat and shut up, I'll pay you a thousand."

"Cash, right?"

"Cash."

"Sure," the driver said and sat down on a bench against one wall. "It's nice and cool in here, anyway."

WORLD OF HURT

Dwayne came awake, still fighting.

His arms and legs were weighted down and immobilized. His mouth tasted like copper. With each breath his nostrils filled with a shithouse stink. His head was a ball of agony, and each beat of his pulse turned up the pain dial.

He opened his eyes to find his entire field of vision filled with the grinning faces of his captors, backlit by the flames of a roaring pyre.

In their large eyes, he saw only deep longing and delight. They pressed down on his arms, and a pile of barking and chirruping brats lay across his legs, their amusement stoked by his struggles to free himself. They were like kids on a pony ride, giggling and whooping. His clothes were torn away. Only his boots and boxers remained.

An adult bastard with a milky walleye sat down heavily on his chest. This guy had red paint smeared on his face. Or maybe it was blood. Walleye lifted a handful of ash and spread it on Dwayne's bare chest over the tattoo there; a garish skull over crossed rifles and the legend: Mess With The Best, Die Like The Rest. He got it one drunken three-day leave in San Diego. He'd always regretted it but never more than now. One of these assholes would be wearing it soon.

The mob crowded all around and grew hushed. They leaned in as Walleye raised a long-bladed flint knife in his fist. Dwayne jerked and bucked, but the fingers gripping him only increased their painful pressure.

Walleye uttered a series of glottal chants and reared back high, both hands overlapped on the knife handle held above his head. His good eye spun in his skull. His muscles tensed for the plunge.

From somewhere high above, there was a whistling sound followed by a pop. The sky turned a brilliant white that washed all shadow and color away in an instant.

The crowd, including Walleye, craned to look upwards. Night had turned to day over the village, and they all gazed transfixed at a single point of light slowly descending toward them. More whistles and pops and the newly-created star was joined by two more. The villagers turned away to shield their eyes, their inhumanly large pupils shrunk to dots.

All around him, hands released Dwayne's arms and legs. The dogpile of brats atop him melted away, and Walleye stood with the others to gaze at the trio of lights drifting down in wobbly progress far above the huts.

Flares on 'chutes. Chaz was back. Dwayne prayed he brought Hell, in the form of Lee Hammond, with him.

Dwayne drove the heel of his foot deep up into Walleye's crotch with all the force he could muster. Walleye sucked in a lungful of air and folded in two. Dwayne snatched the flint knife from Walleye's nerveless fingers. The Ranger was trying to stand and finding it was hard work. The crowd's fascination with the light show waned, and they turned back to their midnight snack. He fought down the urge to retch since standing turned up the pain in his head.

Skinnies closed from all around, feinting and dodging as he

whirled all about thrusting with the knife. He was weak from blood loss or head trauma or both. It was only a matter of time before one of them slipped through his feeble defense or he passed out. His Ranger training in knife fighting kicked in and kept him moving.

A few paces from him, he could now see Jimbo lying motionless. He was stripped to boxers as well. He was filthy and covered in blood drying black on his skin. Dwayne had no way of knowing if it was Jimbo's blood or not. The man wasn't moving. Dwayne made his way to Jimbo's side, jabbing the point of the knife in sudden thrusts to back the skinnies off. They bared teeth at him and hissed. The crowd was seconds from picking up rocks to pelt him and Jimbo to jelly.

A row of skinnies nearest Dwayne crumpled to the ground. The sand and ash all around them kicked up into the air in a sudden storm. Bits of bone and blood spattered the mob. They fell back more in confusion than fear. It was a What-The-Fuck moment for them and wouldn't last long.

Another spray and Walleye was flung to the ground, a lifeless sack of bones. A spray of black blood exploded from his mouth.

Dwayne heard the burr of automatic fire from somewhere out in the dark. More skinnies crashed kicking to the ground, and more spun away missing limbs and trailing innards. Dwayne crouched low. Someone was expertly working an automatic weapon in close fire support. He wanted to make himself as small as he could until he knew it was clear. He covered Jimbo's body with his own.

Another long burst brushed the packed mob of skinnies back farther. The flares were dying, and in the returning gloom, Dwayne could clearly see the path of white tracers as they strobed out from the dark in shallow arcs.

A second and heavier weapon opened up closer to Dwayne. The ring of skinnies faded back, leaving a number of them writhing on the ground bleeding out. The crowd broke up then and ran in full wailing panic for the protection of the surrounding huts.

"On your feet, Rangers!" Chaz shouted as he trotted out of the gloom, two green-glowing discs where his eyes should be.

Chaz pumped rounds toward the huts from the M-4 rifle in his fists. He unslung a second rifle from his shoulder and tossed it to Dwayne along with a cloth bandolier holding ten magazines.

"You remember how to use that?" Chaz said and dropped to a knee by Jimbo and touched the still man's throat with two fingers.

"Fucking A," Dwayne grunted. The feel of steel in his hands gave him a new surge of strength. He worked the action back to chamber the first round and sprayed the huts with a blaze of fire that was joined by automatic fire from a position to his three o'clock, a pounding noise from that heavier weapon. A Squad Automatic Weapon of some brand was throwing out eight hundred rounds a minute. A weapon with awesome killing capabilities in the right hands. If that was Hammond out there in the dark, Dwayne thought, it was as close to having God on your side as any soldier was ever likely to experience.

A fearful keening rose from the village all around them. Dwayne slung the bandolier over his shoulder.

"Lee?" He nodded toward the source of fire in the dark.

"None other. Cover me while I get Jimbo up."

Chaz lifted Jimbo into a fireman's carry, and they backed away from the bonfire and toward the rock face. Both fired suppression all the way. The skinnies stayed in the shadows barking and hooting. These little bastards were just too damn dumb to be scared.

Dwayne whirled at the sound of a sharp crack echoing from the cave mouth. He ran for the opening as a sudden flash bloomed from the dark interior followed by a second crack.

The derringer. Caroline.

Inside, he found the white-painted shaman lying with the

back of his head blown off, a blood-slick flint knife in the sand by him. The chemical stink of gunpowder hung in the air. The old hag lay by the fire with her throat cut ear to ear. Caroline's still form lay propped against the back wall of the cave in the shadows cast by the fire. Dwayne dropped to his knees and crawled to her.

She stared wide-eyed at the frozen grimace of the shaman glaring sightlessly at her. There was a puckered black hole punched in his face just below one eye. She threw the smoking derringer aside.

"He killed the old bitch and came straight at me," she said and shook herself.

"We're going home," Dwayne said and helped her to her feet.

"We are home," she said to herself. "Just way too early for us."

He helped her toward the cave mouth. Outside, the sounds of the one-sided firefight heated up.

"They're holdin' back," Chaz said. He was on one knee to one side of the cave opening and scanning the huts over the sights of his rifle. To his eyes, through the NOD's lenses, he could see the village as a bilious world of shimmering green and white. The eyes of the villagers glowed silver like countless pairs of coins bobbing as they kept a watch from what they believed was the safety of the dark. He popped a large male through the head, and the field of glowing discs vanished in a heartbeat.

"They were born with night-vision. They're waitin' to see what we do next," he said. "We got to move soon. They're gonna follow us all the way up the mesa. Plenty of choke points on the way, and they know them all."

"This is their hunting ground," Dwayne said.

Dwayne was down by Jimbo who was sitting up now and sipping at a bottle of Dasani. Jimbo winced as the water washed over broken teeth. His mouth was bloody from a long gash in his lower lip.

"You maintaining, bro?" Dwayne said.

"One of those little ankle-biters brought me down with a rock," Jimbo said with a weak laugh and held up a black automatic, his own Browning High Power brought to him by Chaz. "I can move. I can shoot."

Fire from the Minimi swept over the huts, short suppression bursts. Thatch blew upwards and tracers lanced through mud walls.

"We got to move and stay on the move." Chaz dug in his shoulder bag. "Hammond's gonna cover the right side of the east trail to the mesa." He tossed Caroline a t-shirt and a pair of cut-off jeans.

"Your brother sent them," Chaz said.

She stepped into the cut-offs over her boots and pulled the t-shirt over her head. It was an XXL with a silk-screened portrait of Celine Dion emblazoned on it, and it fit her like a mini-dress. Parviz and Quebat. Had to be.

"Lead the way, Chaz," Dwayne said and took up the drag position, covering their six o'clock as they moved around the rock face back to the same path Jimbo and he had taken down on their approach only an hour before.

Hammond moved up to a ledge where he could watch the village from a better firing position. The Minimi was hot in his hands after running several hundred rounds through it. His NOD gear specs revealed the figures swarming between the huts in restless huddles. They weren't yet moving to pursue the rescue group as it climbed the east trail toward the mesa. The flares seemed to freak the locals more than anything else.

The field through which the Rangers and the woman would return to The Now was under an hour's fast hike away. With wounded in tow, it would take half again that time at least.

Maybe two hours. A long two hours. Hammond would dog their flank to keep it clean of attacks.

Eventually, the skinnies would wise up and come running. They were hunters, and they brought down prey by running it to exhaustion then attacking in numbers like aborigine hunters had for tens of thousands of years. The Cheyenne hunting buffalo and deer. Inuit after caribou. Masai stalking oryx. His own ancestors, painted in blue woad, running down elk.

The way back to the mesa top was a winding path through dense pine scrub with defiles and rock formations that would make perfect stages for ambush for the Rangers so long as they could keep the lead. These twists and rocks and deadfalls could just as easily provide bushwhacks for the skinnies if they fell behind schedule. Or if Hammond let the little monkey-ass fuckers get ahead of them.

Hammond was covering the far right of the retreat path and would put a fright into the vicious little men, keep them backed off so the rest could make the safety of the high ground. Chaz was to stay to his left to form a moving enfilade and keep the back trail brushed clean and skinnies away from the escape route.

A knot of skinnies was moving forward along the narrow lanes between the huts. They were running to break out of the village. Hammond shouldered the big gun and sent a stream of tracers down toward them. He walked rounds right into the congested knot. The group scattered, leaving a few bodies behind. More small clutches were running forward and emerging from the village at different points, testing their hidden tormentor. He worked the Minimi from one bunch to another, but more than a few were making it into the brush at the bottom of the hill and below his line of fire.

They knew from the trajectory of the tracers where he was and were moving up the hillside to flank him. If they got between him and the rest of his fleeing brothers he'd be no good to anyone. Chaz was right when he warned Hammond that these little fuckers didn't scare easy or scare for long. His situation was deteriorating fast. Hammond crashed through the scrub to scramble up the hill and get his ass farther above the skinnies and closer along the path of Chaz's line of withdrawal.

As he moved, he could hear muted hooting from the foliage around him. They were letting each other know their positions and would rush him when they determined they had the edge. This is how they hunted. This is how they brought down the monsters they stalked with nothing more than spears and clubs. But Hammond was a new kind of monster.

He plucked an HE grenade from a vest pouch, pulled the ring, and flung it high to his left and downslope. The canister tinked and tonked through pine boughs and went off with a flat, sudden crack. The woods all around went silent. No more hoots and hollers.

That gave the little shitstains something to ponder.

Hammond moved swiftly uphill to a new position to cover the evac trail. As he did, he could hear renewed voices from below calling out, punctuated by the barking of the dog pack. The skinnies gave up all pretenses at stealth now. It was going to be a chase now pure and simple. Run and gun all the way to the evac zone.

Chaz took a knee beside the trail and waved for the others to pass him. The blast of the grenade echoed up to them through the trees. It was a sign that the skinnies had broken cover and were closing on their ass.

Jimbo and Caroline Tauber climbed past him. Dwayne stopped and looked back.

"How long you been back here?" Dwayne said.

"Long enough to double-time to your position," Chaz said.

"We opened up when we saw them getting ready to filet you." His eyes scanned the dark woods crowding in on either side of the trail.

"How long back in The Now?"

"A fucking long six days."

"The field will be closed when we get there," Dwayne said.

"Probably. We hold the mesa until it opens again."

"You already thought of that?"

"Because you taught me to, Top." Chaz spared him a glance. "Stick with Jimbo and the lady. I'm waiting on Lee so I can overlap his fire."

"Don't stay too long. We'll need every gun hand up at the exfil point," Dwayne said and climbed the slope after Caroline and Jimbo.

"Roger that."

Chaz looked over his sights into the dense shadows between the tree boles. A bloom of light flashed down to his right, followed by staccato pops. The dark closed in again and a second shimmer gleamed from a new position closer to him. Hammond was closing the distance, firing suppression as he moved. The skinnies were close and working closer, climbing the hill to get above Hammond and encircle him.

Glassing the left side of the trail, Chaz could just make out humped figures moving between shadows a hundred yards down the trail. He kept the sights trained on them. A shushing sound came up through the low hanging boughs down the trail, a rippling movement closing fast on him.

He opened up with his rifle as a pack of dogs exploded into view and ran to close the gap between them and their prey. They ran shoulder to shoulder, haunch to haunch up the narrow trail. The bullets pounded into the rushing mass in a long burst. The dogs' charge collapsed as a half dozen of them tumbled to the trail.

Chaz stood to eject the magazine and slam in a new one. He

scanned the hill as he drew back the action and let it slam home with a clack. Canine body parts littered the trail below him in a mess that sent vapor into the cooling night air. The whimpers of the wounded rose from the brush.

"Chaz!" Hammond called from somewhere below and right.

"Yo!" Chaz called back. "Movin' to your two o'clock!"

"Contact my ten o'clock!"

Tracers ripped through the trees below him, zipping across the trail in arcing trails of glowing white. They tore into the section of the brush where Chaz last saw movement. Hammond was sweeping the trail. Chaz sent some three-round bursts down and to the left just above where he saw figures humping up the hill. He could hear a bunch crashing through the brush below and moving quickly away downhill. They were discouraged for now. But they'd be back up the trail when it got quiet again.

"Make for Little Rock!" Hammond called when the firing died down.

Little Rock was the formation of boulders that formed the designated one-third mark up the trail through the trees. It was near where they found the kid in the Batman shirt on the first day. He'd walked it with Hammond yesterday back in The Now as they mapped their approach path and withdraw strategy. His contingency plan with Hammond was to use the tumble of boulders as a pre-designated defensive position to cover their fallback if things got tight.

They were puckered-up sphincter tight right now.

Chaz turned and ran up the grade at a sprint, knowing that his brother Ranger had his back. He didn't look back as the Minimi opened up below in long, controlled volleys. Hammond was conserving ammo and, more importantly, trying not to burn out the SAW's barrel this early in the fight.

Priority One, Lee needed Chaz to make that group of rocks and cover the retreat.

Chaz arrived at the rocks bathed in sweat and gasping.

Repoing cars was honest work, but it didn't keep a man fighting fit or Army strong. Chaz bitched at himself for the hundredth time since starting this gig for letting himself become an out-of-shape asshole. He knew Hammond was moving fast below him and probably not even popping a sweat, with a heart rate below seventy even as all the shit came down around him. Back to the gym, back to the track for this proud black man, Chaz promised himself.

But first, they all had to get back to the year they came from and the hell out of this place.

Chaz propped the M4 on a flat section of rock in a natural embrasure. He regained his wind taking long, even breaths. This was the perfect redoubt and covered the hill one-eighty around. It was much like it was when they hiked out and surveyed it yesterday except the rocks were more sharply defined here and now, not worn down by millennia of wind and water. And they had a cover of brushy plants with clumps of yellow berries hanging from them.

Below him, he spotted the intermittent flash of Hammond's big machine gun. Sucker weighed over twenty pounds *before* the fat box mag was attached, but Lee played it like an air guitar. Stick and move. Stick and move. Working his way closer to Little Rock and Chaz's protective field of fire.

Figures moved closer coming up either side of the trail. The skinnies assumed the brush and shadows would hide them. To Chaz, they were plainly visible in a perpetual lime-green high noon. Men with long spears in their hands humped up the trail at a run, with dogs loping ahead of them. They were to Lee's left and were moving fast to cut him off in a wide flanking movement. That brought them squarely into Chaz's arc of fire and clearly defined in the light through the NOD lenses.

Chaz laid the blade of the sight ring on the leading runner and squeezed the trigger. The skinny's head vanished in a red cloud and, as he dropped lifeless to the trail, Chaz laid single shots left and right and brought down two more from a good hundred-yard range. The group leaped and crawled to either side, and Chaz stood to send longer bursts downhill. Their advance was broken up, momentum lost. The dogs stood barking and snapping but stopped their forward progress.

A crunch and spatter of rock scree to his right. He swung his sights to see Hammond pounding up through the trees to the foot of Little Rock, snaking and zagging. A spear flew past the running Ranger followed by a second and third. Chaz emptied the magazine at figures closing on Lee's six. The skinnies scattered back downhill to the cover of the trees.

The bastards were learning. They were using cover. They knew they had the numbers but were growing wary, moving more cautiously.

Chaz marveled at how their *esprit de corps* maintained in spite of taking catastrophic casualties. Either that or their strictly animal instincts had taken over and only rage and hunger moved them. Chaz could dig that. Back to basics. Pissed off with an empty belly.

Hammond scrambled between two upright boulders and up onto an exposed ledge ten feet above Chaz; a natural tower.

"I got this," Hammond called and locked a fresh box mag in place. Then he pulled two frags from his vest and pulled the rings. "Catch up with Dwayne. Make sure they stay on the trail and on route."

Chaz moved without speaking and humped uphill, keeping the formation of Little Rock at his back. A basso thud shook the earth under his boots with another just after. The Minimi picked up immediately in coolly controlled three-round bursts behind him. He climbed upward toward the field of stars visible now through the thinning treetops and the clouds racing east.

Up the trail, Dwayne took point.

He divided his attention among the path ahead, the woods on either side, and making sure the other two kept up. The game trail they were following was the same as the one he and Jimbo took down to their hide above the village. The narrow run was cleared by the passage of centuries of hooves and paws. It led straight up the slope by the path of least resistance. But it was easy to lose where it was overhung by long ferns and heather. It was also crossed by other trails, and the wrong choices led to the ridgeline by more circuitous routes or away to dead ends in the woods. Getting hopelessly lost was a matter of a few paces down the wrong track.

Up ahead it widened where it joined a gouge torn in the slope by rainfall that had rushed downhill in the past. It was a straighter path up to the crest with banked sides where years of runoff tore a path to the sea below.

Caroline was going steady, running on her last reserves of adrenaline. She'd crash soon, they all would. Jimbo was the one slowing them down. He was having problems with his balance and fell to his hands and knees to vomit twice, which only made him weaker. Caroline was supporting him by the elbow and muttering encouragement as they came to where the trail hooked sharply around a deadfall. She held Jimbo's Browning now. He kept letting it fall from his hand. Her lime-washed skin looked phosphorescent in contrast to the black t-shirt that covered her to just below her crotch.

The banks along the gully would hide them from sight but offer concealment for bushwhacks as well. Dwayne looked up and could see more sky through the trees. They were nearing the edge of the tree line and would soon be at the open grassy ground leading up to the field area. There'd be less cover there, but the possibility of ambush would decrease. When it came to range, the rifles gave them every advantage. He could tell from the gunfire and grenade blasts coming from below that Chaz and

Hammond were having a bitch of a time keeping the skinny hunting parties from flanking them. If they were cut off from one another, each little group would be overwhelmed in a hurry. Their automatic weapons wouldn't mean dick if they were surrounded in dense brush.

A whisper of sound ahead. Rock on rock. A tree bough moved out of sync with the others brushed by the wind coming down off the mesa. He took to a knee and fisted his raised left hand, then realized that Caroline might not be hip to Ranger sign language. He held his hand splayed behind him in the more universal gesture for 'stop' without turning to look back. Through the ring sight of his rifle, he scanned the ground above them. He wasn't sure what made him stop at first, but the hair on his arms stood up. Listening hard, he picked up a click of stone on stone. Something was disturbing the rock scree above them.

It could have been an animal. These woods were full of them. Even the super-sized herbivores here were dangerous. Critters that would be skittish at home were aggressive and territorial here. Dwayne recalled thinking what a shitty way it would be to go; gnawed to death by beavers. He glanced back to see Caroline down on her knees six paces back. Jimbo was on all fours by her with head hanging low. Caroline held the Browning like she knew what she was doing.

His ears picked up a new sound, a nattering of voices. They were speaking low from just over a hummock of land where the gully curved up and out of sight. The sounds of movement stopped. Did they know Dwayne and his group were here or did they pick this as the most likely trail up the slope? Either way, Dwayne could try and move around the ambush and risk getting lost or wait on Chaz and Hammond and try to bushwhack the bushwhackers by flanking them.

Waiting for the other Rangers risked letting the skinnies add to their number and holding the high ground by sheer force of numbers. These skinnies must have swung away out of range and sight of the automatic weapons. They probably came east along the beach and climbed up here by the same route in reverse used by Dwayne and the others on their first night here.

More automatic fire from below. Controlled three-round bursts from Chaz's rifle and longer volleys from the heavy gun. The sounds of gunfire were getting closer. They were being herded into a killing box like deer. The group above was getting bolder, no effort to hide their hoots and calls to one another, working themselves up for the kill. But they were sticking to their position rather than moving down to close up the encirclement.

If Dwayne was going to break through, it had to be now before the noose closed on them, and while the area of operations was still fluid. He either had to break the ambush or, at the very least, draw the skinnies away from Caroline and Jimbo.

Dwayne was up on his feet with a grunt and moved forward with his rifle butt tight to his shoulder. Dark shapes appeared atop the hummock of ground above, silhouetted against the scant moonlight. Rocks began falling through the pine boughs around Dwayne. They knew he was here. He pumped rounds at them and saw a shadow spin away with a yip. More rocks rained down all around, but they were throwing blind from shelter, just lobbing stones in their primitive version of suppression fire.

He peered around the shelter of a stout tree bole and let loose some suppression of his own. The rock throwing died away. There were barks and hoots in response as they torqued up their courage again. He moved to a better position on the other side of the trail just as a knot of howling skinnies piled into the trail and rushed down the slope swinging clubs.

A long burst sent three of them tumbling and another sat back on his ass with no head. More stumbled over the corpses as Dwayne dashed for fresh cover. Thrown clubs whizzed past him into the brush. He fired as he moved and dropped another one. The rest turned from the trail to follow him. He moved along the slope to the north, luring the shrieking mob away from the trail and Caroline and Jimbo's position.

Dwayne halted to send bursts of snap shots behind him then returned to race for new cover over the rough ground. The rock scree and pine needles made for uncertain footing, and he slid as much as ran in a crooked course across the face of the slope. Turning back to sweep fire at his closing pursuers, he ran into the trunk of a tree and fell hard to tumble downhill. He came to rest in a tangle of brush. He groped for the rifle, finding the smooth Rynite stock and pulling it to him. Skinnies crashed through the foliage all around him, and he rose to his knees and blazed at the nearest one. The little man was lifted off his feet, and his torso opened up and steaming entrails spilled out. Dwayne ducked a club that streaked by him and raised the rifle only to hear the hammer fall with a click on an empty chamber.

He was bowled off his feet by one skinny and then another. They clawed at him, and he held the rifle stock across his chest to hold them away. Their jaws snapped closed as they nipped at his bare arms. A third skinny joined them and scratched at Dwayne's eyes in an effort to blind him. The weight of the three held him pinned, and he released his grip on the rifle to drive two fast punches into the face of one of his attackers. Blood jetted down his arm, and the skinny dropped away. Another sank teeth into the flesh of his leg above the knee, and the pain was nearly unbearable. Dwayne could hear more feet pounding down the slope to join the fight.

Dwayne felt a warm shower cover him. Two skinnies fell convulsing away from him, their heads spraying blood and gobbets of brain matter. Double-tap head shots. Dwayne kicked the leg-biter in the face, driving the skinny's jaw out of place. He rolled to his rifle as the night filled with thunder and light.

Hammond was standing over him pumping round after round uphill with the calm assuredness of a day at the range. Targets left. Targets right. He gave them all hell.

"Am I gonna have to do all the ass-saving or are you gonna help?" he called out, and Dwayne slapped a fresh mag home in the M4 and fired into the dark.

"Good to see you too, asshole," Dwayne shouted back.

"Where's the woman?"

"Back on the trail."

"Lead me back and I'll cover you," Hammond called and hammered two charging skinnies, dropping them to the ground in a spray of blood and bone. "No more half-ass tactics. It's shoot and scoot all the way to evac."

Dwayne raced along the slope of the hill back the way he came. Lee stayed tight on his six. He doubled his pace as the discharge of a pistol boomed again and again ahead of him.

The Browning.

16

FIGHT OR FLEE

The wounded man by Caroline lay still on his back. His breathing came in weak, rattling gasps. She heard him called Jimbo by the other men. He made choking sounds in his throat.

Caroline put down the handgun to push him over on his side, and he breathed a bit easier.

Gunfire exploded to her right. It had to be the one named Dwayne. He rushed off the trail ahead of her a few moments ago and vanished into the woods, with a mob of aborigines close behind him throwing stones and clubs.

She gripped the pistol and sat listening and watching. The weapon was unfamiliar and alien in her hands. Was she holding it right? She was imitating actors she saw on TV. Was that all bullshit? What about safeties? She knew guns had safeties. Was the one on this pistol in the on or off position? She examined the strange black steel object in her hands but could make no sense of the tabs and levers above the handle.

There were shouts and answering calls from unseen aborigines that sounded close all around. She fought down shivers as she trained the gun up the trail where she expected an armed hunter to appear any second rushing down from the crest of the hill.

A thrashing sound came from the brush behind and below her, and she dropped back on her side and twisted around to see two males from the village stumble across the trail below her. They appeared panicked, and one of them had dark streaks of blood running from his shoulder. The larger of the two looked around wildly, and his eyes quickly found her lying prone on the trail just above him. He grinned and stalked forward, a flint ax held tight in his fist.

Her first shot missed, and she was surprised at the weight of the handgun as it jumped back in her fist. The bright muzzle blast took away her night vision. Her next shot went off by accident when she jerked her hand closed to keep a grip on the butt of the handgun. She was scrabbling to her feet, and a body hit her and drove her down on her back.

Caroline bucked and kicked as a filthy thumb jabbed at her face to tear at the corner of her mouth while another hand pressed her head to the ground. His weight pinned the handgun between them, and she strained to pull it free.

The heavy body stank of grease and feces. The huffing male made sounds like braying laughter as he panted with the exertion of trying to hold her still and tear at her face. She pulled hard and yanked her gun hand free from between their bodies. The barrel pressed tight to the ribs of her attacker, she squeezed the trigger twice, and the hands released her with a jerk.

The weight of the still body was shoved off her. The man the others called Jimbo had braced himself against a bank along the trail and kicked the male away. He looked dazed but was smiling weakly.

"That was badass, lady," he said.

Her attacker lay across the trail. The two rounds had torn his back open as they exited. If it was possible, he smelled even worse now. Farther down the trail, the other male lay unmoving from a mortal wound where one of her wild shots struck him. Caroline looked at herself. She was sticky with blood, but at least it was not her own. Her cheek and jaw hurt where the savage tried to rip the skin off her face. She spat again and again to get the taste of that filthy thumb out her mouth.

She held the gun out to Jimbo butt-first. "Naw." He shook his head with a slow, painful motion. "You're doin' fine."

His head drooped, and he collapsed to his side. Out again.

She whirled, gun up, at fresh footfalls below her. Booted feet.

The black man from back at the cave raised a free hand to her as she stopped on the trail.

"Friend," the man said. He was gasping for air and streaming with sweat.

Caroline realized that every muscle in her body was painfully tensed. She relaxed a bit and suddenly felt tired, more tired than she'd ever remembered being in her life, and felt herself drifting away until strong hands shook her by the shoulders.

"Caroline!" the black man was in her face and shouting. "Time for that later! I need you strong!"

She swallowed hard. She pressed her eyes closed. She opened them again and focused.

"Yes," she said. "I'm all right. You know my name. What's yours?'

"Call me Chaz."

He let the rifle drop in its combat sling and lifted the unmoving Jimbo into a fireman's carry.

"You're a Ranger now," Chaz grunted. "You lead the way."

17

BACK IN THE NOW

The helicopter, a big-ass fourteen-seat Sikorsky, landed in an open area behind the Tesla tower. When the rotors slowed to a stop and the dust had settled, men in windbreakers sprang out ahead of a thin man in his twenties. The thin man wore a summer-weight suit of Italian cut. He gestured to the two windbreakers with an open hand to stay as if they were a pair of guard dogs.

He made his way to the collection of pre-fab buildings beyond the tower to find Dr. Morris Tauber speaking to a man by a car marked Alamo Taxi Service. The car drove away, and Tauber stepped forward to greet the visitor.

"I wasn't expecting anyone," Tauber said. "Gus Martin." The young man extended a hand and crushed Tauber's in his tennis grip. "I'm a V.P. at Gallant. Sir Neal wanted me to deliver the news in person."

"News?" Tauber frowned.

"We're shutting you down," Martin said and looked around at the sad metal buildings baking in the late morning sun.

"But we're in the middle of an exercise," Tauber said.

"You have forty-eight hours to pack up and leave everything as it is."

"That's impossible. I'm not sure what you understand about this facility and our work here, but we still have people in the field. I can't guarantee they'll return in two days."

"Frankly—" Martin removed a pair of sunglasses and placed them on his nose, "—I'm really not up to speed on this. And I don't need to be. My official title is Vice President of Facilities Management, but what I am is a fixer. Sir Neal wants this shut down, left just as it is, and you and your people gone. I'm to see that gets done."

"But the Tauber Tube is a creation of my sister's." Tauber realized how weak the words sounded as he said them. "You can't just take over."

"The 'Tauber Tube' or whatever it may be called in the future is the property of Gallant Industries, Dr. Tauber. It was paid for with corporate funds, along with all the recent extras and personnel you've requested."

"But—"

"Look, Tauber. I don't think you grasp what a total fuckup this little enterprise has been. Your report to Sir Neal was alarming, to put it in the kindest terms. You've lost personnel. Two confirmed dead. More missing and their fates unknown. There will be questions. Criminal allegations. The kind of allegations we can't paper over with ND agreements. We'll be lucky to limit inquiries to state authorities."

"But the Tube is a success. It performed precisely as we presented it would."

"That's the only thing keeping Sir Neal from throwing you to the wolves. Your device may be of some actual value to the company down the road. You keep your compensation package. But your further participation here is no longer required, necessary or welcome."

"This deadline is absurd!" Tauber was shouting now. Behind

him, Parviz and Quebat exited the reactor building. They looked like kids playing at spacemen in their Tyvek overalls and goggles.

"You make it work however you can, Doctor," Martin said evenly, and gestured to the two Iranians. "And make sure those two are far away from here, and any connection to Gallant Industries is erased. They're a walking Homeland Security investigation, and we don't need that kind of attention. Excuse me, any *more* of that kind of attention."

"You're making an impossible demand," Tauber said, but Martin had already turned his back and was starting back to the copter.

"It is what it is," Martin said without turning. "Wrap it up. Pack it up. Get out. Forget you were ever here."

Parviz and Quebat made their way at a brisk walk toward the residence hut.

Tauber stood, hands fisted, and watched until Martin reached the copter and it rose airborne in a storm of dust and grit to bank south and out of sight.

The Iranians were preparing some of their high power espresso when Tauber banged the door open and confronted them.

"No excuses. No explanations. No bullshit. I need the nuke powered up as soon as you can make it happen." Tauber was red-faced and breathless.

Parviz and Quebat blinked at him. "They're shutting us down."

The expresso machine gurgled.

"And I don't think they much care if we have personnel on the other side."

Parviz set down his cup and turned off the burbling expresso machine. He muttered a translated summation to Quebat.

"Doctor Tauber, we will do the very best we can," Parviz said. "We can create a controlled surge of the required levels within twelve hours."

Tauber stared open-mouthed at them.

"I've been asking you for that kind for performance for months," Tauber said. "Now, all of a sudden, you can make max levels inside a twelve-hour window?"

"We were concerned with the longevity of the reactor, Doctor," Parviz said. "If they are ending the project, then our long-term needs are no longer of consideration. We will finish our espresso and perhaps some toast, and then return to the reactor and be bringing it back to the required power levels."

Parviz blinked. Quebat smiled at Tauber. "Well." Tauber sighed. "All right, then."

18

THE MARGINS

Dwayne and Hammond were waiting at the head of the trail as the others climbed the gully to join them. They could hear hunting horns to the north resounding through the woods.

"They're getting their shit together," Dwayne said. "This next part is an easier march, but it's over open ground. From here we just stay close and make for the field area as fast as we can."

Dwayne took command naturally, and the others followed his lead. It was habit as much as a sense of loyalty. Their old Top had seen them out of some really bad shit in the past. If it ain't broke...

"Four of you? There's only four of you?" Caroline said and looked around. Two men in boxer shorts, one unconscious. Two other men armed to the back teeth, but still, only two of them. "This is what my brother sent back to get me?"

"Four of the best, Celine," Hammond said. "Let's wait on the post-game for this, okay?"

Chaz said. "Jimbo ain't getting any lighter."

"You're walking drag, Hammond," Dwayne said and placed a hand on Caroline's shoulder. She didn't seem to notice as she stood returning Hammond's glare.

"Sun's coming up," Chaz said. "Can we move? Now?"

The group climbed over the ridgeline and onto the grassy glacis that led up to the lip of the mesa. There was no cover except for groupings of rocks and patches of low scrubby heather and stunted trees. The sun was rising over the mesa before them, creating the pink dawn light peculiar to desert climes. They humped forward as quickly as they could. Chaz invited Caroline to dig into his backpack as they walked and retrieve a plastic bottle of Gatorade. She sipped at it as Dwayne cautioned her to.

"Take it slow," he said. "Your stomach is empty, right?"

"Yeah," she said. "There wasn't really anything on the menu I cared for."

Hammond walked backward, covering the ridgeline below them with the Minimi. Beyond the tree line, the bleats of horns sounded more frequently. Soon the skinnies would be climbing after them in force, and Hammond watched the ridge and the tree line for signs of the first scouts to come into sight. The skinnies were close but not exposing themselves. They'd developed a healthy respect for their quarry's reach.

A long blast on a horn from the edge of the woods was answered by another ahead of them. "Shit," Dwayne whispered. The group dropped low and, from their vantage, they could see spear points against the dawn sky visible over the waving stalks of grass, dozens of spears between them and their goal. The skinnies were moving to block the path to the mesa top.

"Contact forward!" he called back to the other two Rangers.

"We can't stay here," Hammond said. Still no movement from the tree line.

"And we're running low on ammo," Chaz said. He laid Jimbo down on the grass and trained his rifle on the growing collection of spearpoints gathering two hundred yards before them.

"And they have all the ammo they need," Dwayne said and lifted a handful of stones to let them fall to the tumble of scree at their feet.

Hammond stood without a word and double-timed past the group for the mesa.

"Hammond!" Dwayne called out.

Hammond didn't answer. He just trotted toward the spear-points catching sunlight ahead. Chaz shouldered Jimbo and stood. He started after Hammond.

Dwayne helped Caroline to her feet and walked behind her as they moved over the open ground.

A collective roar went up from the mob of skinnies at first sight of their prey moving toward them through the grass. The hunt leaders blew long bleats through the horns. A thunderous blast emerged from a horn fashioned out of a tusk that had to be supported by two males. It was answered in kind by more horns in the tree line. The strangers were trapped between the two groups with nowhere to escape.

The skinnies began to pound the butts of their spears on the rocks in a ragged rhythm. They were stoking their rage. These strangers killed their chiefs, their shaman, and their witch mother. They'd roast them alive over their firepit and peel their skin away in strips as they crisped. They'd feed their guts to the dogs. Many more of the village would die, but only revenge mattered. The tall strangers would die, and the village would go on.

From their vantage point, the rank of hunters in the grass below the mesa lip could see their brothers already emerging from the shelter of the trees. They would drive the strangers forward onto the waiting spears of the growing mob waiting ahead. The children who accompanied the hunters on the climb up from the beach were already gathering rounded stones in piles. Some stood and clacked stones together over their heads in time with the pounding of the spear butts.

Dwayne turned back to see skinnies behind them, forming a wide half-ring to cut off any sideways flight. They were effectively trapped. The large force above them was cutting off retreat. A growing force below them was driving them forward. The two groups could rush simultaneously and overrun them at any moment. The skinnies had proven that they were willing to absorb punishing casualties and still keep coming on. The only chance for the Rangers was to break through the smaller force waiting ahead of them and gain the high ground of the mesa top.

Their options had shrunk to desperate flight followed, if that succeeded, by a holding action of undetermined length.

The skinnies dropped out of sight as Hammond sent a burst downrange from the Minimi. They were learning. They were laying prone and letting the fire go over them. Spearpoints moved to the right and left, a pincer move to match the one below them. The two arms would meet, and the Rangers and Caroline would be in the center of a tightening circle. The rocks would fly and then it would be hand-to-hand with any left standing and all the advantage to the overwhelming numbers of man-eating sons of bitches.

"Stay tight to me," Dwayne said, and Caroline trotted next to him over the rock and grass behind Hammond and Chaz. The two Rangers on point were firing as they moved up the slope. Dwayne fired a long volley behind them at the pursuers now sprinting from the trees to close the distance between hunter and prey.

The dirt and grass seemed to come to life along one flank of the onrushing skinnies breaking from the tree line. A half dozen fell and the rest scattered. Clumps of dirt flew up in the air. Dwayne looked back in disbelief. His M4 didn't do that. More dust erupted as tracers streaked through the grass and into the skinnies tearing them apart in a bloody spray. Legs, arms, and innards were exploding from the bodies. A long thunderous roar rolled down to them from the rocks along the mesa ledge.

Up on the lip of the mesa, a dense white cloud was drifting away on the wind. From the cloud a continuous stream of tracers swept downhill to work across the ranks of skinnies, sending them running back to the trees in a ragged mob. The tracers followed them the whole way, and Dwayne could see figures tumbled and tossed.

"The Ma Deuce!" Chaz called back. His face was split in a grin.

"Who's working it?" Dwayne shouted. "Who gives a fuck?" Hammond said and stood, firing the Minimi at the confused ranks of the skinnies ahead of them below the mesa lip. The hunting party milled about uncertain of what to do in the face of the approaching Rangers and the spray of white tracers streaking over their heads from the rocks above.

The big fifty cal growled into action again and changed its angle of fire to chew up the ground occupied by the skinnies in the shadow of the ridgeline. The angle was bad, and most of the hunting party was sheltered by the mesa wall. But they didn't grasp what was happening. They wanted to get as far from that terrible chundering sound as their feet would carry them. The skinnies fled from the shadow of the mesa ledge straight into the killing field where heavy slugs the length of an index finger dismembered them instantly. Fish in a barrel. The mob broke up and ran shrieking away to the north and south, clearing a path for the Rangers and their line of retreat.

Hammond unlimbered his shotgun and pumped double-aught into a few holdouts huddled in an overhang. Chaz led the way, and they moved up the slope of broad wash to the mesa top under the protective fire of the big .50 roaring over their heads.

They made it to the field area to find Rick Renzi, in green surgical scrubs and missing half his hair, crouched behind the big machine gun with his hands on the trigger pulls. He stopped when he saw them and lit a cigarette off the hot barrel shroud of the Browning .50.

"You still have my lighter, bro?" he asked.

Caroline nibbled Wheat Thins and sipped Evian while seated atop an ammo crate in the shade of a tarp the Rangers rigged up atop the mesa. She watched Chaz making Jimbo comfortable, propped up and conscious now, and holding a cold pack to his mouth.

There were heavy plastic totes on groundsheets around them. It looked like any other desert camp outing except for the guns and ammo cans and blood.

"Don't drink too much," Chaz said and popped an Evian for Jimbo. "You puke, and you drop your hydration level."

"You carried me all the way up here?" Jimbo said, muffled by the icepack.

"I been carrying your ass for years, my red brother." Chaz washed some cuts on Jimbo's legs with an orange-colored antiseptic.

"You bring my long gun?"

"Yeah," Chaz said. "I packed your Winchester along. Get some rest and I'll break it out for you."

As the sun rose high in the sky, Caroline fought to keep her eyes open. The others were busy with tasks that required a minimum of conversation. Dwayne leaned back on a flat rock, relacing his boots. He wore a fresh set of camouflaged fatigue pants and a clean t-shirt. Hammond lay in a position behind a pile of rocks and scanned the approaches below the mesa with a pair of 30x binoculars. Renzi was busy fitting a new barrel to the big black machine gun on its tripod, a Marlboro pressed in his lips.

A scattering of long brass cartridges littered the area around him. She idly picked up one of them. The base was stamped with US 04. Caroline daydreamed about a team of archeologists digging up these artifacts in a stratum they had no business being in.

"We'll need to clean up here," Caroline said, mostly to herself.

"Huh?" Renzi looked up.

"All of this crap. All of it," Caroline said. "It has to go back through the Tube with us."

"All I want to get back through there is my ass in one piece, honey," Renzi flicked the Marlboro butt away.

She could see it was hopeless. Either that, or she was just too tired to argue. Or just too tired for anything. She closed her eyes, vowing it would only be for a few seconds, and fell instantly into a deep sleep.

Jimbo wiped sweat from his eyes and shook his head before pressing his eye to the cup of the scope again.

"You up for this, Cochise?" Hammond said beside him.

"Just tired," Jimbo said and looked down the scope atop his Winchester, the wood stock warm and comfortable against his cheek. He was prone by Hammond, who sat up spotting for him through the binoculars.

"Downrange about three hundred plus," Hammond said. "A few ticks right of that clump of greasewood."

"Don't have it yet," Jimbo said. All he could see was rock and scrub down to the tree line, the ground dotted with the dark shapes of the skinnies brought down that morning. Birds had swarmed down into the no man's land and were gathered around the corpses in amorphous black clumps. More dark shapes circled overhead.

All afternoon they listened to the bleat of horns from the woods. Some kind of jungle telegraph was heating up. Or maybe the skinnies were just bored off their ass waiting on the sun to go down and the hunt to begin again.

"Sounds like a soccer crowd in Somalia," Chaz said.

"Skinnies are skinnies no matter where you go," Renzi said.

"That's racist, dickhead," Chaz said.

"Fuck you, Reverend Sharpton. Far as we know those monkey motherfuckers down there are white," Renzi said.

Chaz had to laugh at that.

Jimbo raised up on his elbows to look over the open sights to find the copse of clumpy bushes. He dropped his eye to the scope cup and scanned over with the 30x. The stand of brush popped close, filling the lens. There was movement there. Two, maybe three, skinnies watching the mesa from what they believed was a concealed position.

"Easy-peasy," Jimbo muttered and let his breath out.

The first heavy round exploded the head of a skinny. Jimbo pulled the bolt back, jacked a new round, and returned his eye to the scope. The second round took another skinny center mass as the sound of the first rifle shot reached them. A third skinny was up and running for the trees.

"He's gonna make that gully," Hammond said, watching the show through binoculars.

"Bullshit." Jimbo slid the bolt home and settled the posts on the back of the skinny who was bobbing in and out of view as he pelted over the rough ground for cover. Squeeze, squeeze, squeeze, and the shape vanished from his view.

"Nice," Hammond hissed. "Dead before he hit the ground. Took him somewhere between thoracic three and four."

"That's pretty specific, Lee." Jimbo turned on his back and rested his head on a rolled-up towel.

"I was living with a chiropractor a year ago," Hammond said as he continued to scan the open ground before the tree line. "She sure straightened *my* bone."

"What made you come on a clusterfuck like this? I can't believe you didn't think Chaz was punking you. A time machine, goddamn," Jimbo said. He was getting his mind off his still throbbing head. The pain in his jaw radiated right around to the back of his skull.

"I could ask you the same thing," Hammond said. "You were working border patrol on the reservation, right?"

"You mean 'catch and release.'"

"That bad?"

"Same shit every day. Same *faces* every day. A guy likes to think he's making a difference. But the rules were written to protect the lawbreakers and lawmakers. Fuck the law *enforcers*."

"The rules of engagement," Hammond said and took his eye from the scope. "That's what I like about this gig."

"There's no rules of engagement here." Jimbo opened his eyes and turned to Hammond.

"Exactly," Hammond said without a change of expression.

———

"You seeing this?" Chaz said and handed the 30x binoculars over to Dwayne.

Dwayne glassed the trees below and could see the smoke of a fire rising from the position where the village lay.

"Look out along the shoreline," Chaz said and placed a hand on the back of Dwayne's head to shift his vision.

"Shit-damn," Dwayne hissed. There were more smoke columns coming from all along the trees at the edge of the sea. It looked like miles of signal fires.

"Reinforcements," Chaz said.

"More like a goddamned surge," Dwayne said and scanned the trees, listening to the growing number of hunting horns.

———

Dwayne tapped Caroline's shoulder gently. She opened her eyes with an effort and slowly sat up. He was offering her a bottle of water.

"You need to drink some more water," he said and crouched by her.

"How long did I sleep?" she said and took a swallow. The shadows were longer and stretched behind them. She turned to where the field would appear when it opened. Just sunbaked rock and dry grass.

"Not long enough," Dwayne said. "But you need to hydrate and try to eat something."

"I just collapsed."

"You don't know the half of it." He laughed. "You napped right through Jimbo firing his cannon downrange all afternoon. Didn't move a muscle."

"You watched me sleep?" she said with a wry expression.

"I checked on you."

"I look like hell," she said. "I itch like hell. All I wanted a few hours ago was a drink of clean water. Now I'd kill for a shower."

"You may have to," he stood and looked west. "They'll be coming once it's dark. If we're still here, it's going to be a long night. Those skinnies own the night. Nocturnal hunters."

"Skinnies?"

"Our hungry little friends," Dwayne said. "Army slang. Goes back to Somalia when the Rangers were in Mogadishu. The locals were skinnies."

"Why do you have to call them anything?" she said.

"You have to call them something," he said. "In your head."

"Well, I guess I've been thinking of them as aborigines. Though that's not strictly accurate. They're hominids of some kind."

"Well, 'skinnies' is shorter."

"But doesn't that demean them? Make you superior to them?"

"They have a name for people who can kill total strangers without reducing them to less-than-human status," Dwayne said.

"What's that?"

"Psychotics." He stood to go.

"You're all Army?" she asked in order to keep him there by her. She didn't want him to walk away.

"All Rangers. *Ex*-Rangers. This is our kind of action. Rough country. Outnumbered."

"How in God's name did my brother find you guys?"

"Friend of a friend." Dwayne smiled. "He's a very dedicated brother."

"Yeah," she said and tipped the bottle. "Let's hope he dedicated his ass to getting the back door open again."

He shook a pair of white pills into the palm of his hand from a small plastic vial.

"Take these," he said and took her hand to drop the pills into her palm.

"What are they? Salt?

"Amphetamines," Dwayne said. "Like I told you, it's going to be a long night."

He watched to make sure she swallowed them and returned to his position along the mesa ledge.

NIGHT FALLS

The blare of the horns increased as the sun fell. There were more of them than before, and it sounded like they were coming from all around. For hours they kept up a continuous ululating noise like a World Cup football crowd, short honks mixed with long mournful tones rising from the woods and rocks.

To the north, the mesa dropped off at a near-vertical angle. The western and southern approaches were long and open—a killing ground. Behind them heading east, the mesa was flat and went on for twenty miles of dry prairie.

The attack lines were clear and predictable. They'd come at a creep or a rush from the tree line. But there was always a chance they'd slip a party up the vertical slope. There was no reason to think the skinnies couldn't climb like goats. They'd seen them scramble up the cliff face above their hometown fast enough.

For that contingency, they set up Caroline in a mini-bunker made of piled totes to keep an eye on the section of the mesa that dropped sharply to the valley below. Dwayne spent twenty minutes showing her how the M4 operated and let her run through a magazine for practice.

"You don't need to hit anything," he assured her. "Just make some noise if you see anyone coming over that ledge. This is a potential blind spot, and we need it covered."

When it got darker, he fitted a NOD set to her head. Dusk turned to noon through the lenses, and the dying sunlight made the face of every rock a mirror. She blinked as she turned her head to look at Dwayne.

"Weird," she said and swallowed.

"They take getting used to. Don't turn your head too fast at first or you'll get nauseous. There's no depth perception. And they're set for 5x."

"Objects will appear closer, right?"

"The opposite of the side view mirrors on your car."

She adjusted the goggles so they sat better on her head and her eyes lined up better with the lenses.

"What you want to watch for is movement," he said. "The trick is not to stare. Just relax your eyes and scan back and forth, but slowly. If anything enters your field of vision, you won't miss it. Movement is the key."

"Like a cat watching a mouse hole," she said and looked at his face, glowing white.

"That's it," Dwayne said and touched her shoulder. "Shoot if you even *think* you see something. False alarms are forgiven in a free-fire zone."

"Is that what this is? A free-fire zone?"

"Biggest one I've ever been in." He smiled.

"Every unfriendly here is *already* dead."

The Winchester boomed and Dwayne moved away to his position, leaving Caroline alone in her hide.

Small knots of skinnies moved out from points all along the tree line. They split up and entered the waving grass in a broad, shallow skirmish line. This was the kind of screening line they used to herd game before them. When those hunters were twenty paces clear more skinnies emerged behind them. The process continued until four ranks of hunters were making their way up the gentle slope to the mesa in a more or less organized line of march.

"Jesus," Dwayne breathed. "There's thousands of the fuckers."

"It's the Little Big Horn," Chaz said, "and we're Custer."

"Not too late to switch sides, Jimbo," Hammond said.

"Go to Hell, white man," Jimbo hissed and picked out another skinny in the NOD's scope.

A hunting chief in a tall headdress of long feathers collapsed backward with half his head gone. The rest pressed forward.

"Light it up!" Renzi called from the .50.

Two flares lit the sky and the ranks crossing the open ground hesitated for just a beat and then rushed forward at a run.

The Ma Deuce roared to violent life and tracers streaked down to meet the first rank in long looping arcs that looked like strings of pearls. Heavy slugs tore a bloody gap in the front wave and created a haze of dust and chopped grass. The second wave raced through waving their clubs and shaking their spears overhead. Renzi walked the rounds down the rank dropping dozens of skinnies with each burst. He was covering the broad path from the open slope to the mesa top and quickly ran through the first 500-round can.

"Feed me!" he called over the cacophony of horns and war shrieks growing louder as the skinnies rushed up the grassy slope. Chaz jumped from his position behind some piled rocks and tore open a fresh can and placed the first round from the belt in the Browning's action. Renzi let the lever go, pressed his thumbs to the trigger plate, and began hammering away again.

The rest worked their rifles with controlled fire. Jimbo used the Winchester to clear the tree line, finding more skinnies moving into the open for a reserve wave.

Dwayne was on semi-auto and picking out individual targets closing on the mesa edge. As quickly as he could pull the trigger, he swung the ring sights to find another skinny and drop them center mass. The ranks were breaking, becoming less organized and the skinnies began to knot together as they sprinted for the rocks just beneath the Rangers for the final short climb. Their discipline was falling apart, but they were still moving forward.

Hammond dropped the SAW and hopped over the rocks with the shotgun in his fists. He leaned out and pumped round after round of buckshot and flechette into a dense crowd of skinnies gathered to clamber up the rocks to the mesa. He couldn't miss if he tried. They fell back screaming in a greasy heap.

"Shoulda brought claymores!" he shouted and thumbed more rounds into the smoking shotgun breach. But you go to war with what you have not with what you *wish* you had.

Jimbo fired another flare off into the sky and laid the scope on skinnies running low along to their right. He nailed three, but lots more made it out of sight to cover around the north face. He swung back to drop a horn blower. More skinnies leaped the twitching form as it dropped into the grass. Beyond the rear ranks, a large untidy mob of skinnies moved from the tree line five football fields distant. Much of this new crowd were juveniles; kids and adolescents anxious to come in for the kill.

Skinnies were now close enough to fling spears up over the mesa edge to land harmlessly on the rocks behind the Rangers. Stones followed and began to clatter all around them. That meant the kids were here and adding to the barrage. Chaz pulled rings from frag grenades and sent them over the edge in underhanded tosses, one following the other.

"Fire in the hole!" he called a half-second before the grenades went off in a close series of thuds that sent a dense cloud of dust drifting over the mesa. The stones falling around them abated but didn't stop entirely. Chaz was struck by rocks dropping on him and pulled the case of grenades farther from the ledge.

The attackers weren't backing down. This wasn't a feint or recon in force. It was a full-on assault—a forlorn hope. The skinnies had never been in a real set-piece battle much beyond a momentary fracas with a neighboring tribe, over before it got started. They knew fuck-all about reserves or tactics. They were treating this like a hunt, and on a hunt, you went all in every time. This rush was their whole strategy. Bring down the prey or die trying.

Caroline fought down her own fear to ignore the sounds away to her left and keep her eyes focused on the length of rocky ledge Dwayne assigned her. She was watching for climbers. She wondered if he really expected her to guard their flank or was finding a kinder way to keep her away from the fighting and out of harm. She also wondered if all his confidence was just a mask for the harder truth. Maybe they were doomed. Maybe they would die here in this strange place so many ages before their births.

Dense shadows were projected from the rocks and brush each time the flares were launched. The shadows imitated movement and made her jumpy. Jumpier, anyway. The M4 atop her stacked-tote redoubt was supported on a bipod mounted at the end of the barrel. She checked again that the selection lever was set to semi-auto. Her hand was slick with sweat and pained her from clenching her hand on the grip. She willed herself to relax, breathe in through her nose and out through her mouth like at her yoga class.

A flicker along the ledge. A sideways movement of light like a crab scuttling back and forth. It was joined by another. She focused through the NOD scopes to try and determine what she was seeing.

They were hands on the ledge, hands of a climber fluttering for purchase then pulling himself up. A head came level with the ledge and then another. A scowling face, ghostly white, was staring right at her. She jerked the trigger and the M4 bucked back, the shot going high. She stood up and lowered the barrel. More figures rose up over the ledge and crouched on the rocks to look for the source of the sudden noise, to look for *her*.

She leaned into the rifle and pulled the trigger three more times. Gouts of sand kicked up in front of the growing group of hunched figures.

"Chill out," she hissed to herself and lined the ring sight up on the lead aborigine who was drawing a flint ax from where it was tucked in a belt tied about his waist. He looked left and right for his attacker. She squeezed slow and even. The round took the aborigine in the thigh and knocked him sprawling. The rest spread out to run out over the mesa top in her general direction. Two of them were running straight for her position. The others were lost to sight either side.

She ignored a spear that whisked past her. She pumped more rounds at the group and another fell back, but the rest moved toward her at a steady pace, mouths working and eyes wide. They had her located and directed their attack to her position.

A hand slammed into her back and knocked her to the ground. The NOD harness flew from her head.

"Stay down!" Dwayne shouted. "Fire in the hole!"

A ping and metallic click followed by a blast that shook the earth under her and warmed the air above her. Dirt rained down on them both. Dwayne's weight was off her and he stood, firing the M4 on full auto.

"Little help!" he called, and she remembered she was part of this fight, not observing it. She found her rifle and sent round after round into the dark, no idea where the attackers were or if her rounds were finding targets.

Dwayne walked toward the ledge swinging his rifle back and forth and firing deliberate shots. He was moving *toward* the danger, not away. She ran to catch up with him. Being close to this big man, so calm in the face of the horror springing up all around, was her haven.

Together they walked and fired all the way to the ledge of rock at the lip of the mesa. She was firing blind and hoping to hit or at least scare something, he was choosing his targets and bringing them down as they either attacked or ran away. She saw the bodies of aborigines, some of them children, lying dead as they moved past. She felt nothing. She caused their deaths and felt not the slightest pang of remorse. Perhaps later, she would.

At the ledge, Dwayne drove his heel into the face of a skinny levering himself up onto the rocks. That sent the red-painted figure screaming down into the dark. Caroline walked rounds down the rocks along the edge to discourage other climbers. Dwayne pulled rings on three canister grenades and dropped them over the ledge one after the other.

"Cover your mouth," he said and ushered her back with an arm around her shoulder. "CS gas."

She could taste a bitter tang in her mouth as a yellowish cloud drifted up from below. Caroline turned away to see the bright flash of the tripod-mounted .50 firing, stabbing into the night in long bursts.

"Toss one of these over the drop every twenty seconds," Dwayne said and pushed a cardboard case of CS grenades into her arms. "And hope the prevailing wind doesn't shift."

"Yes," she said with more confidence than she felt.

"Slow count. Pull the ring and underhand it away from you. Ever play softball?"

"Uh-huh."

"Just like that. I'll be right back," Dwayne said as he moved away. "I have to cover Ricky while he switches that barrel out."

And she was alone again mouthing, "Twenty…nineteen…"

Standing at the head of the broad slope, Hammond fired directly into a mass of skinnies charging toward the mesa top. Jimbo switched to an M4 and was down on one knee adding his suppression to Hammond's. The skinnies climbed over the bodies of their tribesmen to throw spears and axes and rocks.

Chaz and Dwayne carried the Ma Deuce while Renzi followed with ammo cases. They were dropping back to a prepared position, earthworks of sand and rock closer to the field area. Chaz held the super-heated barrel shroud wrapped in a shirt, but he could still feel the heat even through his combat gloves.

They set the big .50 on its tripod and Renzi dropped the ammo cases to begin fitting their last new barrel into the weapon. The current barrel was burnt nearly smooth, and if it was left in place any longer, it would swell and no longer be able to be removed.

Renzi worked quickly to pull the spent barrel out and fit in a new one. They needed the power of the Ma Deuce to hold back the tide. Every second it sat silent the skinnies grew bolder.

"Fall back!" Dwayne shouted to the others, and he and Chaz offered cover fire. Jimbo sprinted back as Hammond rolled a pair of baseball grenades packed with HE down the slope. The blasts tossed a clutch of skinnies and body parts high into the sky. He turned to run, and a spear point struck his back and drove him stumbling to his hands and knees. The spear was deflected by Hammond's body armor, but the hammer shot to his kidneys drove the air from his lungs and made each step agony.

Jimbo was almost to the earthworks and read the dismayed expressions on the faces of his brother Rangers. He turned and ran back to where Hammond was trying to rise with a trio of skinnies almost on him, clubs raised to strike. On the run, Jimbo fired his M4 and took two down with multi-taps to their heads and torsos.

The third skinny fell when Jimbo swung for his head with the butt of the rifle. The buttplate punched a hole in the skinny's temple, and the wound sprayed blood in a shower. Down the slope, the main attack force was recovering from the most recent grenade blasts. They were moving forward in a stumbling phalanx bristling with spear points.

"Off your ass, Lee!" Jimbo hooked a hand under his arm.

"Left leg's numb," Hammond growled.

"Your whole sorry hide is gonna be numb if you don't hustle!"

Together they hobbled to the earthworks under a criss-crossing skein of tracers from Chaz and Dwayne. They dropped flat when the Ma Deuce lit up again. Hammond and Jimbo hugged the ground and felt the concussive wave and flash of heat wash over them from big .50.

"Get your dicks in the dirt!" Dwayne called out between bursts.

The pair crept on their bellies around the earthworks as the .50 hammered at the screaming gang of skinnies behind them. A mob of howling savages drenched red in the blood of their cousins raced to the mesa top and spread out on the flanks. Spears and stones rained down on the Rangers in increasing numbers. It was a steady barrage now with no sign of letting up. More skinnies hauled themselves over the rocks along the ledge and joined a group swinging out to the right to encircle the emplacement.

"Caroline!" Dwayne stood atop the rough earthwork and fired short bursts at skinnies sprinting hard to cut around them. The flanking hunters swarmed into a cloud of yellow vapor billowing before them. They slowed to a convulsing, gasping rabble on hands and knees and rolling on the ground clawing at their own eyes, vomiting convulsively.

Caroline stumbled from the fog with her t-shirt pulled up over her mouth and nose with one hand. She hugged the M4 to her with the other arm and was stumbling blindly. Dwayne rushed out to catch her as she fell to the grass. He grabbed her by an arm and guided her from the cloud of tear gas to the relative shelter of the earthworks.

"Last can for the Ma Deuce!" Chaz called. He was pulling rings from frags and tossing them as fast as caution would allow into the dark around them. Hammond lay propped against a dirt mound and firing a rifle. Jimbo worked the Minimi now. Renzi crouched to transverse the .50 left and right in short disciplined bursts.

Skinnies crowded onto the mesa, absorbing horrific close-range fire and creeping closer over their dead and dying. Some held the bodies of their cousins as shields.

Stones struck all around the Rangers' position. The edge of the cloud of C-4 was carried closer to them on the wind, and the stinging gas was beginning to infuse their eyes and mouths.

Dwayne's M4 clicked empty, and he dropped it to pull a Sig Sauer from his waistband and emptied it at the encroaching mass of hooting skinnies. Despite the hammering they were taking, the horde felt the tide shifting their way. They grew bolder and ran straight into the line of fire to pitch spears over the earthworks.

Caroline sank to her knees as her overheated rifle jammed up, an empty round stove-piped in the action. They'd take her back, and they'd kill these brave men and eat their flesh while she watched. And her fate would be...what? She looked through swelling eyelids to see a handgun lying on the grass. They wouldn't take her. She didn't want to see any more of this world. She just wanted it to end. She reached out for the pistol and felt a chill wash over her as her fingers touched the cool metal.

Dwayne's boot came down painfully on her wrist. She released the pistol, and he reached for her arm to pull her to her feet.

"You feel that?" he shouted with his mouth close to her ear to be heard over the tumult of weapons and voices.

She could see her breath. The chill wasn't fear, it was in the air. The temperature had dropped suddenly and dramatically. She turned to see a thick white mist spreading out to cover the grass all around them.

"The field!" she called back. "The Tube is operative!"

"Fall back!" Dwayne yelled repeatedly and slapped the shoulders of the other Rangers.

Jimbo was up and helping Hammond stand. Chaz was squatting atop the earthworks and had a cardboard carton of frags open. He pulled the ring on the one packed in the center.

He stood and lifted the box above his head. "Heads down!" he shouted and threw the whole damned thing in an overhead heave toward the skinnies rushing closer over the grass.

The resulting blast lifted him on a concussive wave and threw him back over the earthworks where he lay dazed. Renzi tumbled down by him. The carton of grenades went off in a tight sequence of explosions throwing arcs of shrapnel into the massed skinnies and scything them down like harvest grain.

Dwayne hooked Chaz under the arm and dragged him back into the frigid mist with Caroline's help. Jimbo and Hammond stood firing their M4s one-handed, Hammond leaning on his brother Ranger for support.

"Fall back, Ricky!" Jimbo called.

"Move it, Renzi!" Dwayne joined in. "Haul your ass!"

Renzi either couldn't hear them or was ignoring them. He was back up at his post behind the Ma Deuce and pouring tracers downrange at the skinnies trying to regroup there. Empty shell casings tumbled to the ground at his feet with a clatter.

Dwayne took a step to join Renzi, to force him to surrender his position and join them in retreat. Renzi turned his head to look back, an unlit Marlboro clenched in his teeth. A wild berserker look flashed in his eyes. It was exhilaration. It was madness. His breath came in vapor in the chilling air as he barked a laugh. He turned away to swing the big .50 back and forth at the closing pack of naked fiends.

Caroline yanked hard at Dwayne's arm, and he moved to her to help her pull Chaz into the spreading cold, back to a world they knew. Back to The Now.

WHAT GOES AROUND

Caroline was the first to emerge from the field, and Doc Tauber left the control array to meet her with a crushing embrace. He held her tight to him on the metal walkway until they were separated and shoved clear by the rush of Rangers moving from the Tube.

Staggering, Chaz dropped Hammond to the floor. Dwayne and Jimbo took up positions at the foot of the ramp and trained weapons into the Tube.

"Renzi!" Dwayne called into the mist. "What's going on?" Tauber said. "You left someone behind?"

"We were on the run, Mo," Caroline said. "It all went wrong out there."

A figure was moving swiftly out of the mist in the Tube field. Tauber stood frozen to stare at a squat man who raced from the fog. He was swinging some kind of stone-bladed ax over his head. His body was smeared in red, and his face painted white. A roar rose from his wide-open mouth and filled the Tube chamber. The animal sound was drowned out by rapid explosions from Dwayne's rifle. Jimbo joined in as three more naked men leaped into view out of nothingness. Their lifeless bodies tumbled to the foot of the walkway, spraying blood.

"Renzi!" Dwayne took a step forward, and Jimbo grabbed his arm to stop him. "We have to go back! We can't leave him!"

A rock sailed from the mist to bounce down the walkway. More followed it, making a metallic racket on the floor plates and railings. Dwayne and Jimbo fired into the Tube field on full auto. Chaz joined them with the Minimi and the barrage of stones died away.

"They overran him!" Jimbo held Dwayne's arm and turned him so their eyes met. "We'd walk back into a shitstorm and die back there with him!"

Dwayne stared wild-eyed at Jimbo. His mouth worked, but nothing came out.

"Priority one—hold our ground!" Jimbo shouted and increased the pressure on Dwayne's arm. "Ricky bought us time! We have to use it!"

Stones and spears began flying from the bone-chilling fog again. More humped figures came into view shrouded in the vapor pouring from the coils, bare feet pounding forward on the plates.

The Rangers opened up, pouring fire into the mist, murdering any shape that made itself visible in the narrow confines of the Tube. A heap of bodies grew within the field. Hot blood struck the ice-rimed coils and boiled away. The men kept up the continuous fire, pausing only to slap in fresh magazines.

The deep hum of machinery died away, and the giant fans in the walls and ceiling activated to pull the cold air from the room. The mist dissipated to reveal a pile of bullet-riddled bodies lying whole and in pieces on the frost-covered walkway. All of them were skinnies. The back wall of the chamber was punched full of holes from the Ranger's final volleys as the Tube shut down and the gateway to the past vanished.

Dwayne dropped to the floor to sit where he was, the last

stores of will and the dregs of the amphetamine rush drained from every muscle. In contrast, Jimbo stood pumping his rifle in the air and letting loose a wolf howl that echoed around the big room. Chaz leaned on the railing on the walkway and grinned.

They hadn't forgotten the man they'd left behind. They just surrendered to the heady elation of having survived despite shitty odds. Exhaustion, fear, and blood loss took their toll. They were left helpless to their own animal physiology. There was plenty of time for guilt and recrimination later if they could still feel those things. For now, there was no room for anything but joy.

They were the baddest motherfuckers in the valley and, damn, it felt good.

Caroline stood and returned her big brother's hug. The tears came. The harder she cried, the harder she held him to her, as if afraid he might vanish and she would open her eyes to find herself back in that horrible cave.

***

Six showers later her skin still felt gritty even though she had scrubbed her skin red. Her hair was still stiff though most of the lime had been washed away. For a fleeting instant, she considered shaving her head.

Morris met her as she exited her bathroom wrapped in a thick robe. Her brother sat on the edge of her bunk and held out a cold bottle of Fiji and a paper cup filled with capsules and tablets.

"You need to take these," he said.

"Mo..." she moaned and shooed him from the bunk so she could lie back, propped on pillows.

"It's your own protocol, Carrie," he said and handed her the cup. "Antibiotics, antifungals, antiparasitics, minerals, vitamins, and a strong laxative."

"Ick," she said, then popped the pills and sipped water.

"I thought I'd lost you," he said.

"You worry too much," she said and washed down pills.

"Actually, I *knew* I lost you."

"What's that supposed to mean, Mo?"

He told his sister of finding the cave and, with Parviz's and Quebat's help, uncovering a skull that was undeniably hers—a skull with a bullet-sized hole in it.

She shivered and took a long pull of Fiji. "I'm just too damned tired to get my brain around that right now," she said and laid back. The pill cup was empty.

"It could be a confirmation of string theory," Morris said. "If we could publish about it. Which we can't."

"That doesn't mean we can't explore it further. I can already think of some simple experiments." She allowed herself the luxury of closing her eyes for a few seconds.

"Yeah. It does mean that, Carrie. They're shutting us down," he said.

"Who? What did you say?" She sat up. "They're coming tomorrow. Some corporate hard case named Martin. He says Sir Neal wants us gone. I nearly fried the system getting it powered up this last time to get you all back here before the deadline."

"This work is mine. Yours. They can't just take it."

"Same old story, Sis." He frowned. "Our work. Their money. We signed agreements. We were both so fixated on seeing your theories realized that—"

"We'll build our own Tube," she insisted. "I already have ideas for improvements, ways to make it work more efficiently."

"Well, unless you're holding a winning lottery ticket..."

"Where are my clothes?" she asked emphatically and pointed at a trash bag tied shut by the door of her room. "There! Tear that open."

She stood over Morris as he worked at untying the bag. Caroline grabbed the bag, pried her fingers through the plastic, and ripped it open to dump the stinking mess on the floor. She dug through the sweat-soaked and bloodstained t-shirt and came up with the necklace Old Mother had put around her neck back in that forgotten time.

She held the necklace of black claws up to Morris, and he recoiled at the musky odor of it.

"See that?" she held between her fingers a dull yellow bead set on the necklace thong between the claws.

"That looks like gold," he said and removed his glasses to squint at it.

"How far back in that cave did you dig, bro?" A broad grin wrinkled her nose.

Men trotted out to meet the helo as it landed. They were big men. Their suits were expertly tailored but could not hide their nature. These were soldiers and moved with the assured confidence of men used to standing their ground when others fled for cover.

"They've vacated, sir," the tallest of them said as Gus Martin stepped from the copter. He changed to cross-trainers on the ride from Vegas. The last trip out here had ruined the custom loafers he bought in Parma last winter.

"Really, Bohrs?" Martin said in mild surprise. "I thought they might stay behind and make me listen to more of their wretched pleading."

"There are a few unexpected items we found in our initial inventory," Bohrs said and walked beside Martin down to the compound with a pair of Martin's aides following behind.

"I hope there's nothing that will complicate our deal with the Chinese," Martin said. "They're coming tomorrow for an inspection of the property and a brief demonstration."

"There was a considerable amount of spent brass on the floor in the main building," Bohrs said. "And some minimal damage to the structure, but the mechanism appears to be intact."

"Brass?"

"Ammunition shell casings, sir. Lots of them. And quite a bit of blood evidence, which led us to the grave."

"Grave." Martin felt a migraine building behind his eyes.

"A mass grave with multiple bodies," Bohrs said. "They used a backhoe. We partially uncovered the remains."

They reached the compound area and the three black Suburbans that had brought the Gallant security men there that morning. No other vehicles were here, but there were broad, deep tire tracks in the sand.

"A semi-tractor trailer, sir," Bohrs said as Martin stopped to look at the fresh ruts that led away from the huts down to the service road.

"They didn't have a truck the last time I was here," Martin said.

"We think they used it haul the reactor away," Bohrs said.

Martin turned to the reactor hut and noticed for the first time the ten-foot-wide hole roughly cut through its steel outer wall. He snapped his fingers, and an aide handed him a satellite phone. Martin punched a series of numbers and held the phone to his ear.

"Sir Neal, if you please," Martin said blandly.

A pause as a voice replied.

"Then, you'd better damned well wake him up," Martin's voice dropped to a chilling rumble. "He insists on good news fast and bad news faster."

The story continues with Blood Red Tide, book two in the Bad Times story from Chuck Dixon.

Treasure is *when* you find it.

The Rangers have returned from the prehistoric past to find themselves in an even more dangerous time---the present.

Being on the run takes money. On the run from the richest man in the world takes millions.

From a forgotten cave in the Nevada desert to the pirate-infested seas of the ancient world, the Rangers hunt for treasure lost to time. The travelers to the past find once again that history is not what it seems and the future is always in doubt.

Available now at Amazon and through Kindle Unlimited.

AUTHOR NOTES

JUNE 2, 2019

Thanks for picking up this series.

The origin of these stories begins on the living room floor of the house I grew up in. The very first stories I created were with toy soldiers and sometimes I'd have to mix historical periods in order to create battle scenarios. A few times plastic dinosaurs joined the melee! And that's really where *Bad Times* began. When I went to create a brand new set of stories I decided to indulge those adventure fantasies of my childhood in a time travel epic featuring a cast of the toughest, most resourceful soldiers I could think of. I hope you enjoyed these novels and are looking forward to future (or past) trips into the Tauber Tube.

Chuck Dixon

ABOUT THE AUTHOR

Chuck Dixon is the prolific author of thousands of comic book scripts for *Batman and Robin, the Punisher, Nightwing, Conan the Barbarian, Airboy, the Simpsons, Alien Legion,* and countless other titles.

Together with Graham Nolan, Chuck created the now iconic Batman villain Bane. He also wrote the international bestselling graphic novel adaptation of J.R.R Tolkien's *The Hobbit.*

His first foray into prose, the *SEAL Team 6* novels from Dynamite Entertainment, have become an ebook sensation. He currently scripts *GI Joe Special Missions* for IDW publishing as well as the *Pellucidar* weekly comic strip for ERB Inc.

He calls Florida home these days.

You can connect with Chuck here:

Facebook:
https://www.facebook.com/chuck.dixon.779

Website
http://dixonverse.blogspot.com/

Amazon
https://www.amazon.com/Chuck-Dixon/e/B001HOL26O

www.ingramcontent.com/pod-product-compliance
Lightning Source LLC
Chambersburg PA
CBHW050137110726
47898CB00008B/2566